WHITE COOLIES

Authors note

4 5 6 - 1 8

23, 24, 25

BETTY JEFFREY

WHITE COOLIES

GEORGE MANN • MAIDSTONE

Betty Jeffrey

WHITE COOLIES

First published in the United Kingdom by
Angus and Robertson, 1954

This edition first published 1973

ISBN 0 7041 0017 7

Printed by Lewis Reprints Limited, Tonbridge
for George Mann Limited, 40 Bower Mount Road, Maidstone,
in the County of Kent

To
those nurses who did not return

AUTHOR'S NOTE

THIS is the story of those Australian Army nursing sisters who were in Malaya with the 8th Division A.I.F. in 1941 and early in 1942, and were later taken prisoner by the Japanese.

The Australian Army nursing sisters in Malaya were evacuated in two groups a few days before the fall of Singapore. One ship, *Empire Star*, left Singapore on 11th February 1942 with the first group of sisters and, after being constantly attacked from the air by Japanese bombers, reached Batavia and finally Australia.

The second group of sixty-five nursing sisters left Singapore at 6 p.m. on 12th February 1942 in the *Vyner Brooke*, which was bombed and sunk by the Japanese two days later. Of the fifty-three survivors who swam or floated ashore twenty-one were murdered by the Japanese and the remainder were taken prisoner.

The following story was written periodically by one of the surviving sisters, while prisoner, during the next three and a half years.

FOREWORD

By COLONEL A. M. SAGE, C.B.E., R.R.C.,
Formerly Matron-in-Chief of the R.A.A.N.C.

THIS is a story of women who fought in the last war. Yes! I mean fought, for they surely did, just as surely as the sailor with his submarines and guns, the soldier with rifle and tank, and the airman with bombs and machine-guns.

With these women, it was a different kind of war.

They fought against anything which threatened to destroy life. Theirs was a courage not stimulated by the lust for battle, but born of women's natural instinct to tend the sick, the helpless, the suffering and the fearful.

They were the Nurses! Three and a half thousand of them served with the Australian Army Nursing Service (now the Royal Australian Army Nursing Corps) and in this story Sister Betty Jeffrey tells of the experiences of some who were taken prisoners of war by the Japanese.

What they suffered physically was almost inhuman, but only woman can fully appreciate their terrible mental anguish and constant dreadful fear of what the Nipponese could and might do to them.

The terrifying experience of Sister Vivian Bullwinkel, the sole woman survivor of the Banka Island massacre, and her subsequent behaviour, have earned for her acknowledgment and admiration in all English-speaking countries of the world.

This is a story which should be read and remembered, not only for the fine examples of courage and bravery of which it tells, but also for the grand humour, resourcefulness, and ability to overcome the greatest of problems, and withal, to keep morale at the highest imaginable level.

This is so typical of the Army Nurses. I had the privilege of seeing them in many places. I saw them in the desert, in the jungle, and on the high seas. I saw them housed in tents or huts and menaced by all the terrors of war as well as by the scourge of malaria, scrub typhus, and other tropical diseases. The longer the war progressed, the greater grew my admiration for them. I will never cease to love them all.

No greater compliment could they receive than that paid by the late Field Marshal Sir Thomas Blamey when he referred to them as "A magnificent Service".

AUSTRALIAN ARMY NURSING SISTERS, PRISONERS OF WAR, ABOUT WHOM THIS STORY IS WRITTEN

2/10th A.G.H.

Blake, K. C. (Pat)
Blanch, J. J. (Blanchie)
Davis, W. M. (Win)
Delforce, C. E. M. (Del)
Doyle, J. G. (Jess)
Freeman, R. D. (Dot)
Greer, J. (Jennie)
Gunther, J. P. (Pat)
James, N. (James)
Jeffrey, A. B. (Jeff)
Mittelheuser, P. (Mitz)
Oxley, C. S. M. (Chris)
Singleton, I. (Rene)
Syer, A. C. (Mickey)
Trotter, F. E. (Trot)
Tweddell, J. (Tweedie)
Woodbridge, B. (Woodie)

2/4th C.C.S.

Gardham, D. S. (Shirley)
Hannah, E. M. (Mavis)
Raymont, W. R. (Ray)

2/13th A.G.H.

Ashton, J. C. (Jean)
Bullwinkel, V. (Viv)
Clancy, V. R. (Veronica)
Harper, I. (Iole)
Hempsted, B. (Blanche)
Hughes, G. (Gladys)
McElnea, V. I. (Vi)
Muir, S. J. (Sylvia)
Oram, W. E. F. (Wilma)
Short, E. M. (Shortie)
Simons, J. E. (Elizabeth)
Smith, V. E. (Val)

Chapter I

It is October 1942. From the doorway of this small three-roomed cottage, which houses thirty-two of us, we look out beyond to a steaming jungle in Sumatra. And sometimes we look back along the long trail that started so undramatically from Melbourne one midsummer day last year, and led us to this, which has been our lot now for the past eight months.

So, too, I write in retrospect—keeping a watchful eye out for the Japanese guards who wander in and out of our houses all day with fixed bayonets—with a precious stub of pencil in an exercise book I managed to scrounge from the guard-house.

When we sailed from Melbourne to join the 2/10th Australian General Hospital in Malacca there was no war in the Pacific. When it did come, dramatically, on 8th December 1941, we were right in the thick of it. Early in the New Year the Hospital was forced to evacuate to Singapore. We took over a Chinese school and turned it into a hospital. Later we expanded into a neighbouring guest-house, then occupied private homes near by as the owners evacuated them.

Here we worked, under continuous daylight bombing raids, while the situation grew more tense daily. By 10th February it was obvious that matters were working up to a climax. Six of our sisters had left earlier at an hour's notice in a Chinese Hospital Ship, taking many patients with them—but not enough. At breakfast that fateful day Matron Paschke was informed that the hospital was surrounded by Japanese. We looked like being taken prisoners at any moment, but there was not a sign of panic. We finished our meal, put on our red capes, and with small week-end suitcases, greatcoats, and hats walked from our quarters to the main hospital and got on with the job.

About 10 a.m. came a summons for about thirty sisters to leave immediately. A ship[1] was available and was to make a dash for it.

Poor Matron! What a decision she had to make! In her usual calm manner she assembled as many of us as she could, then simply divided us into two groups—those on the one hand to go, those on the other to stay. There was no time for anything else—and everyone wanted to stay and carry on. But off they went, under orders, with hardly anyone to see them on their way. We were flat out receiving wounded, and still more wounded, while the bombing and noise went on and on.

On Thursday there was worse to come. Matron drove Sisters Halligan, Cuthbertson, Blanch, Davis, Freeman, and myself over to our other hospital on the next hill.

Never had I seen such a sight. There were wounded men everywhere—in beds, on stretchers on the floor, on verandas, in garages, tents, and dug-outs. Low-flying planes were machine-gunning all around us. They just cleared the roof and trees, but did turn off their guns while passing over us, starting to fire again immediately they left us behind. We had rigged up a large red cross on the front lawn with white sheets and yards of red material Matron had obtained.

[1] The *Empire Star*, which sailed early the next morning (11th February).

2

At 1.45 p.m. Matron made us stop working and have lunch. Just as we started a car arrived. It was to take us to the wharf at Singapore, about three miles away. There were only six of us.

We all flatly refused to go. There was so much to be done. Wounded were arriving constantly; no hospital ships were in Singapore to relieve the congestion. Our two-hundred-bed Manor House hospital, with the smaller homes, was rapidly approaching the one thousand mark.

But our refusal was useless. We were ordered to leave and had to walk out on those superb fellows. All needed attention; not one complained—doctors, too, who needed our help so badly. I have never felt worse about anything. This was the work we had gone overseas to do. We sat in that car quite dazed by the suddenness of it all. Back at our main hospital we were transferred to ambulances and joined a convoy of all the remaining sisters.

We got under way at once, taking only what we could carry. An orderly threw my half-filled kitbag to me—what a pal! The last person I saw was a doctor with the same name as mine, standing there waving and wishing us luck. I shall never forget the expression on his face.

We drove through an air raid into Singapore by side tracks. Japs were everywhere and the main road was taboo. Once we took cover—in St Andrew's Cathedral. It was a queer sensation, sitting in that huge cathedral seeing the rows of Army sisters—some wearing captails, some in tin hats, one or two with outdoor felt hats on (we had all been on duty)— sitting quietly while an air raid raged and ack-ack guns echoed loudly through the church.

A list of our names and numbers was taken. How many hundreds of similar lists have since been taken by the Japanese? Later we were joined by the remaining sisters of the 13th A.G.H. and the 2/4th Casualty Clearing Station, whose names and numbers were added to the list. We now numbered sixty-five.

When the all-clear sounded we were driven to the wharf.

Singapore seemed to be ablaze. There were fires burning everywhere behind and around us and on the wharf hundreds of people trying to get away, long queues of civilian men and women, and a long grey line—us. Masts of sunken ships were sticking up out of the water, but no ships were in sight other than forlorn-looking barges.

As we walked along the wharf we noticed that dozens of beautiful cars had been dumped in the water; some were smashed on top of each other, others were visible only by a wheel or part of the engine sticking out of the water. Cars during that last week in Singapore were literally given away as people evacuated; these obviously were scuttled to prevent the Japanese from using them.

While we waited for our ship another air raid started. This time the ack-ack guns were alongside us—terribly noisy things which made the tin roofs of buildings near by rattle and rumble.

At last we were on the move—into a tug which took us down harbour to a small, sinister-looking dark-grey ship, *Vyner Brooke*, flying a naval flag—a white ensign, I think. Before the war she had been privately owned by Sir Charles Vyner Brooke, Rajah of Sarawak.

Much to my relief, we were told to live on the top deck— I loathe cabins and ships' insides!—and after a "meal" of dry biscuits and bully-beef we were under way, just as darkness set in. It was a never-to-be-forgotten scene—huge fires were burning along the whole front of Singapore and the black smoke billowed higher and higher far behind the town.

We soon settled down to sleep on the decks with our coats over us and gas respirators for pillows. During the night at sea guns fired from ships and searchlights flashed; we must have been on the outskirts of a small naval battle. Next morning we learnt that we had lost our convoy during the night and got lost in the minefields—thank Heaven we didn't know that at the time!

This day, significantly, was Friday, 13th February. We spent it keeping our fingers crossed and hiding behind islands, stopping all the time. We all kept wishing we could get on with the journey we were supposed to be making towards Java. And the noise of battle rolled not so far away.

That night we anchored again. Progress was so slow that by 2 p.m. next day we had travelled only 160 miles from Singapore. It all seemed so futile. If we were evacuating Singapore, why spend days and nights anchoring alongside the most inviting beaches?

How Pat Blake and I longed for a swim as we stood leaning on the deck rail! We did not know just what a long one was in store for us before the day was out.

As food was short we decided not to have lunch, but to rest instead. At 2 p.m. we were wakened by the ship's siren from the first decent sleep we had had for at least a week. Aircraft overhead. No doubting whose—those horrible red spots told the story. We had to don lifebelts, tin hats, etc., go down one deck and lie on the floor of the lounge (right under the bridge) and wait, while the six planes collected themselves into formations of three and proceeded to bomb us.

We had a view—too horribly clear—of it all. First time they missed, but she was a very small ship and the near misses made her rattle. She zigzagged just in the same way as a ship we had seen being attacked off the Malacca Swimming Club two months before. On that occasion the ship was not hit.

I felt certain that the bombs would miss us, too. We were able to relax a little while the planes gathered themselves together to try again, but it was nerve-racking, really, waiting. And it was most uncomfortable on the floor. There were about two hundred people on board, far too many for so small a ship, which didn't leave much room for my long legs, and I always seemed to have a small child's feet under my tummy.

The poor little kid was wonderfully brave. She didn't utter a sound. Her mother had four small children with her and she calmly prayed aloud—the Lord's Prayer. Poor soul, if anyone needed help she did.

Back came the planes . . . and this time we were just about

lifted out of the water. The little ship shuddered and rattled.. There was a terrific bang, and after that she was still. No more zigzagging. A bomb hit the bridge. Another went straight down the funnel. For a minute the place was blacked out. We were told by an officer to "stay put", so, moving Hazel's foot to another part of my tummy, I chatted with Sister Ennis about "near misses".

Down the planes came again, and what a crash! It felt as if the bomb had landed right in the room with us. Then shattering glass, tons of it, smoke, and the sounds of crashing walls.

We had been given instructions that morning what the drill was to be if we were bombed or torpedoed. Different jobs were allotted to each nurse. Now everyone hurried about the decks doing the task assigned to her.

We were all carrying morphia, field-dressings, and extra dressings we had made on board. Sister Ennis and I made a bee-line for the bridge, being last down into the lounge. Taking a child each with us, we were first out. We left the children with an Englishwoman and dashed towards the bridge, only to find it was an unrecognizable mess and burning fiercely. I grabbed a Malay sailor and put my inadequate field-dressing on the worst part of burns on his leg. It was an emergency dressing I had brought all the way from Melbourne and carried around Malaya for nine months!

Even this critical time had its lighter moments. During the scramble to get up on deck and to the lifeboat stations a woman's high-pitched voice called out above the din, "Everybody stand still!" It had an amazing effect. Immediately there was dead silence. Everyone stood unmoving. Then the same voice came again, "My husband has dropped his glasses." This eased the situation and there were gales of laughter—but the glasses were not found.

We had been told to see that every civilian person was off the ship before leaving it ourselves. Believe me, we didn't waste time getting them overboard! Nobody was anxious to linger on a burning and rapidly sinking ship.

6

But the planes had not finished with us. Over they came again and machine-gunned the deck and all the lifeboats—rather effectively. The ropes holding the three lifeboats on our side were severed. Two dropped into the sea. One filled and sank, the other turned upside down and floated away. The third was already manned by two Malay sailors and I'm sure they never anticipated such a quick trip down. I couldn't help laughing at the expressions on their faces as they hit the water and found that their boat had filled almost immediately and left them.

Beth Cuthbertson searched the ship when it was at a very odd angle to make sure all wounded people had been taken off and that nobody remained, while other nurses were busy getting people into the sea.

At this stage there were quite a few people in the water—including the ack-ack crew, who had been blown there with the first bombs—and the ship was listing heavily to starboard. The oldest people, the wounded, Matron Drummond and some of our girls with all the first-aid equipment, were put into the remaining lifeboats on the starboard side and lowered into the sea. Two boats got away safely. Greatcoats and rugs were thrown down into them and with bright calls of, "See you later!" they rowed away. The last I saw of them, some sisters were frantically bailing out water with their steel helmets.

The third boat was caught by the ship when she started to roll on her side and so had to be evacuated very smartly.

Matron Paschke set a superb example to us all by the calm way in which she organized the evacuation of the ship. As the Australian sisters went over the side, she said, "We'll all meet on the shore girls and get teed up again."

It was our turn. "Take off your shoes and get over the side as quickly as you can!" came the order. Off came our shoes—I'll never do that again; I am still shoeless—and we all got busy getting over.

One sister thought the order silly. "I'll drown anyway, as I can't swim," was her comment as she went over in her

7

shoes. Sixteen hours later she landed—in her shoes, and she still has them.

It was wonderful to see the way those girls jumped over or crawled down rope ladders into the sea. They made no more fuss than if they had been jumping into the swimming pool at Malacca.

Land was just visible, a big hill jutting up out of the sea about ten miles away.

I had been so busy helping people over the side that I had to go in a very big hurry myself. Couldn't find a rope ladder so tried to be Tarzan and slip down a rope. Result, terribly burnt fingers, all skin missing from six fingers and both palms of my hands; they seemed quite raw. I landed with an awful thud and my tin hat landed on top of me.

What a glorious sensation! The coolness of the water was marvellous after the heat of the ship. We all swam well away from her and grabbed anything that floated and hung on to it in small groups. We hopelessly watched the *Vyner Brooke* take her last roll and disappear under the waves. I looked at my watch—twenty to three. (Most of our watches are still twenty to three.) Then up came oil—that awful, horrible oil, ugh!

I was swimming from group to group looking for Matron Paschke, who that very morning had jokingly asked me to help her swim for it if we had to go over the side. Nobody had seen her leave the ship, so I went on searching wherever I saw groups of girls in grey uniform. I met Win Davis and Pat Gunther clinging to an upturned canvas stretcher and stayed with them for a while, then went on again through that revolting oil when I saw a raft packed with people and more grey uniforms. There was Matron, clinging to this crowded thing. She was terribly pleased with herself for having kept afloat for three hours, and as she was no swimmer I quite agreed with her. Never have I met such an amazing spirit in any person.

On this raft were two Malay sailors, one a bit burnt, who were ineffectively trying to paddle the thing, but had no idea

8

how. Sister Ennis was holding two small children, a Chinese boy aged four and a little English girl about three years of age. There were four or five civilian women and Sisters Harper, Trennery, and McDonald from the 13th A.G.H., Sister Dorsch from the 2/4th C.C.S., and Matron Paschke and Sisters Ennis, Clarke, and myself from the 2/10th A.G.H. There seemed no hope of being picked up, so we tried to organize things a little better. Our oars were two small pieces of wood from a packing case and nobody seemed to be able to use them to effect, so more re-arranging was done. Those who were able hung on to the sides of the raft, those who were hurt or ill sat on it, while Matron, Iole Harper, and I rowed all night long in turn. Iole was wonderful, when not rowing she would get off, swim all round, count everybody, and collect those who got tired of hanging on, making them use their feet properly to assist in pushing the thing along.

We seemed to pass, or be passed by, many of the sisters in small groups on wreckage or rafts. Everybody appeared to be gradually making slow progress towards the shore, and every one of us felt quite sure she would eventually get in.

The last thing we saw before night fell was the smoke from at least five ships on the horizon and we thought we were saved. Surely this was the British Navy? Later on we saw motor-boats searching for people in the darkness; we shouted to them, but they missed us. We eventually came in close to a long pier, but were carried out to sea again. We saw a fire on the shore and knew the lifeboats had made it, so we paddled furiously to get there. We gradually got nearer and nearer and saw the girls, even heard them talking, but they could neither hear nor see us because of a storm, which took us out to sea again. We tried again; it was a lighthouse this time, but once more we missed it by a narrow margin. We seemed helpless against those vile currents. A ship's officer floated past us sitting on a piece of wreckage; he told us where to go when we landed and wished us luck. We didn't see him again.

The two small children with us were very good and they slept most of the time in Sister Ennis's arms. It was very rough and dark and we rocked and tossed until everybody was sick. During this storm the little girl awakened and her tiny voice said, "Auntie, I want to go upstairs." Poor little soul, she was absolutely saturated with salt water, but Ennis had to take off her pants before she was convinced that it would be all right. Those two children behaved extremely well, cried very little, and were certainly no trouble.

We came in towards the lighthouse again and I suggested to Matron, "Let's give her twenty and we'll make it." We nearly did, but the currents wouldn't let us, and out to sea we went for the third time. We saw large rocks ahead and paddled over, but to our amazement found them moving slowly towards us—ships! As the first went slowly past us we had to push ourselves off from its sides with our feet and the oars. There was no light nor any sound of life at all as they stopped. From the third ship came many large motor-boats, each one packed with armed Japanese soldiers; they surrounded us, chatting away, then one boat came alongside —what an awful sinking feeling we had! They looked hard at us, spoke to us in Japanese, then away they went in a fan-shaped formation towards the town of Muntok. All this left a pretty awful taste in our mouths, for we then realized we didn't have a chance of getting away from them at this stage. We were told that the Japs didn't take prisoners. . . .

When daylight came we were all very tired and just as far out to sea as we were when bombed, but miles farther down the coast; beaches had disappeared and all we could see was a distant line of tree-tops and what looked like jungle. Behind us were about fifteen ships, some of them firing guns towards Muntok.

As we were not getting anywhere and the load was far too heavy, the two Malays, Iole Harper, and I left the raft to swim alongside and so lighten the load. My hands were badly cut about now and too swollen to even cling to the ropes, also we were too tired to row any longer. Two other sisters took over and at last we made progress. We were all coming in well, we four swimming alongside and keeping up a bright conversation about what we'd do and drink when we got in—then suddenly the raft was once more caught in a current which missed us and carried them swiftly out to sea. They called to us, but we didn't have a hope of getting back to it; they were travelling too fast for us to catch them. And so we were left there.

We didn't see Matron Paschke and those sisters again. They were wonderful.

Chapter 2

WE didn't see the two Malays after about an hour—they just disappeared.

I kept my eye on Iole as she got farther away from me. My stinging, swollen hands were nearly driving me crazy and my progress was very slow. Iole was visible only as a blob about four hundred yards away. Now and again there would be a white blob and I realized then that she was turning round looking for me. I waved; she waved back. Then the blob was black again, going on its way.

Iole was swiming thus away and ahead of me in a different current and so reached the trees first—no beach, just mangrove swamps. She was there a long time before I arrived, which was well after midday. We could tell that by the sun, and we both went to sleep immediately, hanging on to a dead and leafless tree, our bodies still floating in water that was well out of our depth.

Later we discussed our prospects of swiming to Australia!

We spent the remainder of that day swimming up creeks and down again—because they all ended in dense jungle. Our progress was slow, for we had to swim breast-stroke. Thank God we had lifebelts, though the canvas had already rubbed our chins raw. The peculiar animals, crabs, and fish we met along the way didn't exactly inspire good cheer. We would be swimming along through these swamps, when suddenly something would go flop into the water beside or behind us. And fish would go flipping along the surface of the water in an upright position on their tails. If only we could get along at that rate!

In the late afternoon the tide went out, leaving exposed sharp mangrove roots and long hard spikes, which cut our hands and legs still more and our tummies until we were just about at screaming point.

But there was one humorous interlude. Iole was about fifteen yards ahead of me when suddenly she turned round and called out, "Oh, by the way, what's your name?" We had been swimming together for twenty-eight hours!

So we paused, while we formally introduced ourselves, looked each other over, and exchanged names and addresses. As we belonged to different units we had never met before. She was a little person, about five feet high, had very wet, short black curly hair and the smallest and prettiest hands I had ever seen.

The water was far too salty to drink; we were swimming up the creeks to see if we could get to fresher water, for we were beginning to get thirsty. There was no sign of land or civilization.

When it was dark the tide was right out, and we couldn't make any further headway, sinking in mud up to our thighs. Once when I was sinking in that slimy soft mud and my legs and arms had disappeared in it, I suddenly saw ahead of me very plainly the white sheepskin mat in front of the fireplace at home—I also saw my father sitting in his armchair with a

Herald over his face, asleep. He has often done that. It certainly made me snap out of it and get free of that patch.

We crawled and scrambled through this to a dead tree-trunk and climbed to the top of it, where there was just enough room for us. We sat there changing places every few minutes because we were getting numb. Huge birds flew at us hitting our faces with their wings—they were horrible.

Soon the tide rose again and we kept on moving to stay out of the water, because it was still dark. During the night Iole kept pointing down at the oily black water and saying to me, "There are the beds, why don't you get into one?"—and was furious when I refused. I could see Sister Win Davis giving an orderly a glass of water and asking him to bring it to us; I saw this every time I closed my eyes for the next two days, so perhaps I was just as crazy as Iole. I know we were both terribly hot.

When the water reached us we floated off and swam all that day, pausing only to watch planes dog-fighting overhead. We must have swum many miles that day towards the beach at Muntok. We saw a few crocodiles. Late that night we found a river—a big one this time—so we swam up until we were too tired to swim any farther. Then we found something that looked like grass, so we got out on to it. It was grass, but very squashy. We broke palm leaves with our elbows because our hands were too badly infected and made a bed there. Then we heard a dog bark; we were thrilled to know we were on the right track at last. Again we had to keep moving, for we kept sinking in the mud and we were smothered with mosquitoes and sandflies. There must have been thousands of them! While there we heard the splash of oars. We rushed to the water again and called to two natives in a small boat, but they didn't take the slightest notice of us.

During the night we heard some animal coming slowly towards us, snapping dead twigs as it came. We were scared stiff. Then two large eyes appeared above us; it sniffed us all over, and—thank Heaven—went away again.

Again we heard dogs barking and knew we must be near

a native village and decided then and there to swim on up the river. We got back into the water and later heard the Malay fishermen coming back in their boat. They called to us and paddled alongside, all smiles, and helped us into their boat. What a relief after three days in the water! We produced our scanty Malay, asking for a drink of water and food; they smiled and nodded, and everything seemed to be pretty good.

We went quite a long way upstream with them, and eventually reached their village. First thing we noticed was a row of thirteen sharks lying on the ground to dry! We were taken to the fisherman's hut, where we sat in the kitchen —after he had put the fowls outside—and dried ourselves by a stove. His wife and a small boy gave us cold tea first, then made us a pot of hot tea and some small hot cakes, which we ate as they came out of the oven. I haven't tasted anything better since!

We were then taken on to a veranda where the whole village had collected and they stood there and stared at us and talked amongst themselves. They were most concerned about our cuts and infected hands and legs and kept pointing to them. Then a Chinese appeared, dressed in spotless white pants and shirt, looked at us for a while, and said, "Good morning."

What a relief to find somebody we could talk to! He introduced himself—he was from Singapore, had been taken prisoner and escaped, and was trying to get through to Java. He told us where we were and that the island we were on, Banka Island, was in Japanese hands. We knew that, of course —almost helped them take it! He was a bit shattered to hear we had been swimming since Saturday. It was then Tuesday. He said the natives wanted to look after us, but suggested we give ourselves up, since there were quite a few white people in a native jail in Muntok who had been taken prisoner.

We sat here until a Malay girl named Johanna came along with a bowl of hot water for us to bathe our hands and legs. She then bandaged them for us and later returned with sandals for us. We were soon removed to the native temple and told by the Chinese to wait there until the Japs came. He then disappeared as quietly as he came. Some dear old Malay man came along and presented us with an opened tin of Australian preserved apricots, and another with some rice and cooked fish. It was beautifully cooked; we ate until we couldn't eat another thing.

It was in this temple that Iole and I discovered that our sisters were friends and neighbours at Somers, Victoria, both being married to officers in the Royal Australian Navy. We soon felt we had known each other for years.

In a little while a truck drove into the village. It seemed to be smothered with Japs, so we got up from the seat on which we were lying and walked out to meet them. Horror of horrors—they jumped off the truck and ran towards us, fixing their bayonets to their rifles as they came! We were too dazed to do anything but just stand there while these bayonets rested on our stomachs—actually on the button of my belt, which made the shank stick into me. It hurt quite a lot, so I moved the bayonet down a little.

We got on very well with these fellows; they spoke fluent Japanese and we spoke in our very best Australian, and after five minutes had not got anywhere, so showed them the map of Australia on our buttons. They screamed at us, "Americano! Americano!" and they took a lot of convincing that we were not Americans but Australians. After a lot of by-play they bundled us into their truck, allowed the Malays to give us some coconuts, and drove us off.

As soon as we got round a corner they immediately changed their attitude towards us, removed their bayonets, put their rifles down, and offered us cigarettes and small packets of biscuits. A few miles farther on they stopped again, made us get out, changed their minds, made us get in again, then gave us a cup of water each.

After bumping round the roads in the sun and dust for about an hour we drove into Muntok and were taken to a house which appeared to be a temporary headquarters. We were given a chair each and told to sit on a veranda, where we watched a Jap take a machine-gun to pieces, clean it, and put it together again. I couldn't bear to watch it, so turned in my chair and dropped my head on my arm. Next thing I felt a hand on my shoulder and we were both motioned inside. I was quite sure they were going to shoot us and followed the machine-gun, but was very relieved to find it was for lunch. *Quite* a relief! We were given a whole tin of bully-beef and some dry biscuits, with a fork, which was an after-thought on their part, but we couldn't eat a thing. They insisted on our drinking hot milk and water. An officer tried his best to be decent to us, but we just couldn't understand each other, so he sat there and smoked and smiled to cheer us up a bit. Later on he took us to a room where Japs were lying on a floor, clad only in G-strings, and made us show them what to put on their wounds. We could do nothing, since our hands were smothered in bandages.

A little later we were taken outside by a guard and we tottered down a road in the blazing sun for some time until we came to a queer-looking jail place, and in we went. Two women dressed as Malays in sarongs were near the door. We were walking past them and one called to me, "Jeff!" To my surprise and relief I recognized two girls from my unit, Sister Jennie Greer and Sister Beryl Woodbridge. It was wonderful to know that somebody else had come in out of the sea.

We went inside and were surrounded by other Australian sisters. I walked past another Malay and to my amazement she said, "A bit haughty today, aren't you, old thing?"—another of the nurses I hadn't recognized. They were all so sunburnt, and every one of them had the same raw chins as we had, where our lifebelts had rubbed.

Iole was taken off by her friends from her unit and we all met again in the dormitory—and how we all talked!

These sisters all had terrible tales to tell of how they eventually got ashore from the *Vyner Brooke*. Some landed on the pier, the others were scattered for some miles along the beach and walked towards the pier. They were taken prisoner there and herded with hundreds of other people in the Customs house and later on in a cinema, where they spent two awful days before being marched out of town to this place, a native jail, where they were installed when Iole and I arrived on the scene.

Chapter 3

We were now thirty-one—thirty-four still missing, including some of the sisters who passed us on their rafts. We discussed those missing to see if we could account for them all. What had happened to the people and our girls who left the *Vyner Brooke* in the lifeboat in charge of Matron Drummond? From the sea some of us had seen them land on a beach and later that night had seen them grouped round a fire, but they had not turned up. We heard an ugly rumour which we refused to believe.

The sisters were all dressed in sarongs and badjus or navy or army shorts, white or khaki, given to them by some of the prisoners. What an odd-looking crowd we were!

Iole and I were both washed and had our hands and legs again cleaned up and bandaged and were given an injection by an English woman doctor. Then we went to sleep, and slept for hours.

Later we looked round us. The coolie jail was a concrete quadrangle with an iron roof and dormitories at each side. To rest we had to lie on concrete slabs side by side, like sardines in a tin. Forty of us to each dormitory, twenty lying abreast on each side. This is where we learnt to sleep on unadulterated concrete and to eat filthy rice!

At the foot of the dormitory ran a deep concrete drain, which was the lavatory. It was awful, just a gutter, no protection, no privacy, and used by both the Japanese and us. The air was putrid.

Water for drinking came from one tap, which could only drip. There was a constant queue the whole time waiting for some. Bath water trickled into a large concrete trough called a tong, and we stood here and whisked a tiny amount of water over ourselves for a bath.

There were about six hundred people here—nuns, civilian and service men and women and children, survivors representing about seventy odd ships that were sunk that week in Banka Strait. There were quite a number wounded, so the nurses got busy and cleared one dormitory to use as a hospital. There were three women doctors, two British and one German, and with a good supply of nurses things were soon under control. There was no soap at all and only one towel.

For two weeks I couldn't help at all, my hands seemed to be stuck shoulder high and for the life of me I couldn't put them down, so I had to be washed and fed by my friends.

Wilma Oram was walking about the place doing her job of nursing with an awful looking scalp wound on top of her head. She informed me that a raft fell on her head while she was swimming away from the *Vyner Brooke* and sent her under the water. Each time she came up to try again another raft hit her. In all, six rafts hit her—she must have the skull of an ox! Wilma was telling me how Veronica Clancy arrived in the Customs house to be taken prisoner. With complete nonchalance she strolled in, dressed in her corsets and a man's overcoat! It must have been a sight, for Veronica is a big girl. She had used her uniform as a sail and brought a raft in that way.

We were fed on rice twice a day, the drill being to line up in two queues, men in one, women in the other. We would stand for hours, it seemed, with the tiny Chinese bowls we had found, and then get our ration—a spoonful of the most evil-looking rice I had seen, grey and burnt. The first meal was at midday, the second at 4 p.m. At midday we sometimes had a little sugar, which helped considerably, otherwise we were given some salt. With this we were given a cup of luke-warm fluid called tea, but it tasted like nothing on earth. At 4 p.m. we had "stew", which consisted of the same awful rice, with perhaps a piece of vegetable, possibly potato, the size of a threepence, or perhaps a tiny pink splinter, one to each bowl, which we were told was pork. Sometimes we had what was called coffee, which to my way of thinking was the best drink of the lot. There was a faint resemblance to the real thing.

There was nothing to do all day long but walk up and down or play bridge. We had one pack of cards between us, good-ness knows where they came from.

We went to bed about 7 p.m., always hungry, for the rice satisfied us for only a short time. I have never seen such sights as the Australian Army Nursing Service putting itself to bed! A mixture of old pants, sarongs, cast-off pyjamas, old frocks and bits of old material swathed round our per-sons—anything that would cover and protect us from the swarms of mosquitoes. It was also very amusing to see the way the girls settled down to sleep on the hard, cold concrete—and was it cold and solid! Our bones seemed to freeze all night. Guards walked in and out all night long to make sure we wouldn't sleep, and flashed their torches on us or hit us on the legs with their bayonets. Why, we didn't know. Another little game was to turn all lights on in the middle of the night, and when all the camp was awake and babies crying they would turn them off again.

One day someone found a mattress, so five of us settled

down on this—Win Davis, Pat Gunther, Jess Doyle, Pat Blake, and myself. It was a bit of a bun-fight with all the wriggling that went on and it wasn't such a huge success after all. However, we didn't have it for long, because some very sick English nursing sisters came in one night after being on rafts for five or six days, so we gave it to them. They were badly shocked and sunburnt, but soon recovered.

About a week later another Australian sister arrived, alone —Vivian Bullwinkel. We were terribly relieved to see her, and she was just as relieved to see us. We hoped this meant that the others might gradually come in, but this hope was dashed when we heard her story.

Chapter 4

VIVIAN is a tall, slim girl, with very fair straight hair, cut short, and blue eyes. She is not an excitable person at any time, and she quietly walked in through the door of the jail, clasping an army-type water bottle, which was slung over her shoulder, to her side. We immediately saw why she did this. It was hiding a bullet hole in her uniform.

We took her into our dormitory, and as we all gathered round her she told us what had happened.

Vivian was with a group of servicemen, civilian women, and twenty-two Australian Army Nursing Service sisters. They had all gathered at this one spot on the sandy beach about two or three miles from Muntok, and had come ashore in lifeboats or had swum in. They spent the first night sitting round the fire we had all seen from the sea. There were quite a few wounded people with them, so they decided that when morning came they would search for some Japanese and see if the wounded could be cared for properly.

They waited all day, but nothing happened, and when night fell they were still there.

Next morning it was decided that a naval officer should walk into Muntok and bring back some Japanese with stretchers for the wounded, also informing them of the presence of the party on the beach.

After an hour or so of waiting the civilian women decided to walk on to Muntok themselves and so meet the Jap party on the way along. Our sisters, with Matron Drummond of the 13th A.G.H. in charge, stayed behind to look after the wounded members of the group.

A little later the naval officer returned, bringing a party of Japanese with him. To everybody's amazement, the men were then separated from the nurses and then taken along the beach round a bluff and out of sight.

Later the Japs returned, wiping their bayonets, and everyone realized what had happened to the men.

The nurses were told to form a line, including the wounded, and walk into the sea. They were then machine-gunned from behind. All were killed outright but Vivian. A bullet passed through her left side just above her hip and sent her headlong into the water. She floated there for some minutes, then, when the Japanese had gone away, was able to struggle ashore. She realized she was the only person to survive. She wandered into the jungle, lay down by a tree, and went to sleep.

As soon as Vivian was able to walk she went back to the beach, thinking it was the same day and she had been asleep only a few hours. On the way she found an English serviceman, who told her he had been lying there for two days. His arm was badly wounded and he had been bayoneted. She helped him to move into the shade of the jungle, then went off to look for some food and water. She found a stream and was able to bring back water in her bottle.

For about ten days Vivian looked after this sick man, going each day to a small native settlement and getting food from them and water from the stream. The natives told her to give herself and her companion up to the Japanese; they had seen white women wearing Red Cross arm-bands in Muntok. They did not want to help them. As both were feeling a little better they decided to do this and so they set off for Muntok.

On the road they heard a car coming and it tooted at them. Quite unconsciously they moved to the side of the road to allow it to pass, then it dawned on them that the car must have Japanese in it, so they waited. It pulled up and a Japanese naval officer motioned them to get in. They did so, and he gave them a banana to eat.

This officer took them to Naval Headquarters and questioned them, then later brought them to the jail to join the rest of us.

What a wonderful relief it must have been for that poor girl, only in her twenties, to see familiar faces after going through a hell like that!

Vivian's companion was desperately ill and was put into the crude hospital here. He died a few days later.

After we heard this story we decided then and there never to mention it again; it would not do for it to go back to Japanese ears. The subject was strictly forbidden.

Chapter 5

A FEW days after Vivian arrived we were all taken from Muntok across Banka Strait and sixty miles up the hot Musi River to Palembang, Sumatra. It was 2nd March 1942.

We were told the evening before that we were to be ready to start at 3 a.m. It didn't take long to pack our belongings, so we were first ready. We were given a small bowl of rice for breakfast, and then a handful of cooked rice wrapped in a piece of banana leaf, looking quite revolting, and two tiny biscuits some of the women had cooked the previous day. This was our ration for the day.

It was still quite dark as we started off in a long, dreary line through the town to the pier. My hands were still bandaged and useless and were still held up high, but Win Davis arranged our gear so I could carry a bundle under my arm without using my hands at all. Iole's legs were still stiff and bandaged and she had a most painful journey. At last we came to the pier and we walked and walked. We are all sure Muntok has the longest pier in the world—how we missed it that night on the raft I don't know. To our surprise there was nothing resembling a ship at the end to take us across to Sumatra, so we sat there until dawn, then we noticed a few awful old ships about half a mile away. We waited about an hour or so, then two small launches appeared, manned by two Australian men and one Jap guard, and we were taken, about twenty at a time, to the dirtiest old tramp thing, where we sat on the deck or on a pile of wood and watched the most perfect sunrise we had ever seen, complete with a double rainbow. Women and children only in our ship, the men travelled in a larger one that followed us.

Soon after daylight we started off across the Strait (twenty miles of it) and into the Musi River. The farther we went the hotter and stickier we became. There was no protection from that hot sun, not even a hat; then it poured with rain, and we got drenched. When the rain was just about finished the guards produced some old and dirty tarpaulins for shelter. Then the sun came out again and we stifled. By the time we reached Palembang at 4.30 p.m. we were a very sorry crowd. Nearing Palembang, we were interested to see the river was thick with oil and the banks very singed. There was a huge oilfield near by. Two ships were sunk, one rather large one, which was sideways on, blocking a large portion of the river.

The lavatory on our ship was rather a crude idea. It was an ordinary wooden apple case, with middle panel missing, nailed on the back of the ship and sitting perilously over the propellers. To make matters worse a Jap guard, complete with fixed bayonet, sat near by; we wondered what he thought he was going to do. Of course, few people were brave enough to step over the side into the box, though many desperate souls tried.

When we tied up we were taken off along a very narrow plank at a very tricky angle, and were left sitting on our miserable wet bundles on that wharf until about 6 p.m. I think each one of us felt like the original wreck of the *Hesperus*. I wouldn't know how many times our photographs were taken by the Japs. We were hungry, cold, and tired.

At last we were moved off towards some open trucks and were driven at furious speed, standing up and being booed at by the natives, through the town. So out to a native school. We still don't know why we didn't turn over going round corners on that drive.

We were welcomed to this school by British and Dutch servicemen. It was good to see them, and we all heaved very weary sighs of relief when they informed us that they had a hot meal and hot tea ready. It was stew—potatoes, spinach, and other oddments in hot gravy, and it was excellent.

We were divided into groups of forty to each room, and put ourselves to bed as quickly as we could, lying in rows on the cement floor. An electric light glared in our faces all night long. We never looked like going to sleep with that light and the mosquitoes and children and babies crying. Those poor mothers!

In the morning we were a very odd-looking crowd, our faces had swollen and our eyes were almost invisible.

We sat around this place all day, while the servicemen, Air Commodore Modin in particular, tried for hours to impress on the Japanese officers that we thirty-two were military personnel and should be treated as such, or at least be near the servicemen. But it was of no avail and we were marched away during the afternoon, with a very mixed crowd of civilian men, women, and children of all ages and colours. After a long walk we eventually came to some houses and were told to go inside. We thirty-two had two houses allotted to us, but two Dutch homes separated our houses from the other people. There was very little furniture, one double bedstead, quite bare, a few chairs and a small couch, but what thrilled us was an electric stove! This was much more than we expected. So we settled in.

On two or three occasions some Dutch people called, bringing hot soup, a few toothbrushes, and odd things that were very necessary, since we really didn't have anything between us. It was a great help to know we had friends outside the barrier who were not afraid of the Japanese.

Rations improved for the first two weeks. We were given green vegetables, mostly a type of spinach, and a daily ration of our own army biscuits! Two or three times a week pork arrived, but the Englishman who acted as rations officer didn't think we needed any, so we had pork twice in the first month. It was useless making a fuss about it; he was far too friendly with the Japs and was a very poor type.

Then the fun started again. The two Dutch houses separating us from the rest of the camp were evacuated. We were very sorry when these Dutchmen went; they had been very good to us, and had managed to get a little bread and sometimes cheese over the fence to us on odd occasions. We sisters then had to move into these two houses so that the Japanese officers could run a club in the two houses we left. A Japanese officers' club right next door to us—we didn't like that.

It was a Sunday and pouring with rain when we transferred furniture, precious electric stove, and everything we could lay hands on, over the fence. The team-work was excellent, one person every yard as it was all passed down the line and over the low concrete fence.

Chapter 6

ON Saturday, 14th March, we first heard of the part we were to play in the club. Next day it was confirmed. We had to "entertain" the officers. Opening night was to be Wednesday the 18th.

We felt sick; we couldn't eat. We were told that if we refused the whole camp would have to go without rations for four days.

We went without rations for four days. Again the Dutch came to our aid. A Dutch doctor was able to get in a small sack of flour to each house (it was Australian flour!). We had a good time with that flour, making scones and dampers, and fried scones and pastry with pork fat, and generally ringing the changes. This was better than the eternal rice.

On Wednesday morning half a dozen of us were ordered by the Japanese to go and scrub out three houses in a street over the way from here. We immediately called it "Lavender

Street"—a reminder of Singapore—when we were informed it was part of the club and was to be used that night.

Later in the day some of our girls were told to go next door into the club, each one alone. As the Japs had a list of our names, all they had to do was to send for, say, Sister Davis. Win went—and returned ten minutes later in a fury. She was so furious she could hardly tell us what had happened before another message came, for Sister Blanch this time.

Apparently they had to stand before a few Japanese officers, read something on a paper, then answer questions.

Win read, and said, "No."

"You do not know what you say," said the interpreter.

"No. No," said Win. "N — O spells 'no'."

"But why not, sister?"

"No," said Win.

"You will die then."

"I would rather be dead at your feet than do this," replied Win, and walked out of the place.

The other sisters in their turn did likewise.

Of course this thing had to be thrashed out, and some of the opinions expressed are worth mentioning.

One sister said she wasn't going to be a plaything to all and sundry in the Japanese Imperial Army; if the worst came to the worst she was going to concentrate on one man, preferably the doctor.

Another girl thought it might be a good idea to teach them to play cards! Somebody else suggested we should all swear never to mention it, or tell any tales about anyone if and when we were released.

Another sister sat on, in her calm and unruffled way, and said, "What is to be will be."

However, 8 p.m. that awful Wednesday came and a message arrived for us to sally forth over the fence. Two Englishmen, a Mr Tunn and Mr Stevenson, were most concerned about this and tried to help us, but they felt they could do so little. However, they wouldn't leave us alone with the Japs. One stayed in the first club house and the other stayed in the second, as barmen, to look after us. They were simply wonderful and their presence bucked us up no end.

The first thing we noticed on entering this, our late "home", was a picture on the wall of a pure white lily! Somebody had blundered! It did not make us feel any better. I have not seen the Australian Army Nursing Service at a party in such outfits. We wore what we had left of our uniforms— no collars—our footwear consisted of sandshoes, football boots, men's shoes, while some of the girls were barefooted —a most unattractive sight as everybody sat round the room. No powder, no lipstick, and quaint hair-do's. We had trouble getting Pat Gunther ready, the more she plastered her curly hair back the prettier she looked. The rest of us looked awful.

After a while six of us were asked to go into the house next door, so about fourteen of us took off and positively staggered two Japanese officers. After they recovered from the shock at the sight of us they were reasonably decent. They gave us soft drinks prepared by Mr Stevenson, who whispered to us, "Keep it up girls, you're doing well."

We had there our first and last taste of proper biscuits and salted peanuts.

We must have been a formidable-looking crowd. They wanted to know why we didn't have powder and lipstick, and would we like to go into town and buy some?

No, thank you very much.

They also wanted to know what girls in Australia drank on Saturday nights! We told them milk. But it didn't do any good, we didn't get any.

About ten o'clock their English was exhausted, and so were we, so they sent us home.

All but four girls in the first house were sent home, too. These four were not so fortunate.

They had to go out of the club, each one led by a Japanese officer, who tried to get them across to the houses in Lavender Street. The girls refused to go and kept them walking up and down in front of our own houses for some time until the whole eight of them were exhausted wrecks. At last one girl had a bright idea and began coughing. She was dropped like a red-hot coal—the Japs are scared of T.B.

After an awfully anxious hour they came home. We all talked long into the night. What could we do about the situation?

We didn't sleep properly for weeks. The next week was too awful to write about; we refused flatly to go near that place again. I really think the mental strain was far worse than being bombed and shipwrecked. Eventually our Dutch doctor friend reported these goings on to the Japanese Resident in Palembang. The club was suddenly stopped and peace reigned for a couple of weeks.

Rumours then started that we were to be moved to Singapore at any moment and many long and varied discussions took place all day as to whether we wanted to go or not. Could we nurse our own soldiers in Singapore? Or could we nurse the servicemen here in Palembang? All this didn't get us anywhere and life went on.

The only bright piece of news was given to us one day by Mr Tunn. He told us he had just heard over a radio that sixty-five Australian sisters, who had been evacuated from Singapore a day or so before us, had arrived safely in Australia. We all cheered—thank Heaven those girls got home!

We had nothing to do and all day to do it in. We decided to break open a small store-room at the back of this house we were in. We found a R.A.A.F. greatcoat, no name on it, no clues whatever, and a great heap of papers and Dutch magazines on the floor. We had a good laugh, anyway, as somebody found an old *Australian Women's Weekly* amongst the magazines. Inside this we read an article and saw photographs taken in our own hospital unit in Malacca some months before. We did look well dressed then—shoes! stockings! capes! captails! starch!

Chapter 7

On 1st April we were rudely awakened very early and told to pack up and be down at a "padang" about half a mile away, within half an hour. We raced about the place trying to pack so as to carry as much as we could. It broke our hearts to leave the precious stove. Two Japs sat on the couch and watched the proceedings, and kept nagging at us to hurry. Trouble was, we could find nothing to pack our things in. Another Jap sat on the fence outside and had the nerve to whistle "Home, Sweet Home".

Once more a long dismal-looking line of us moved down to the padang, which was rather a pretty park. After all our hurrying in the house to be there in time we had to stand and wait in the blazing sun, hatless, until about 2 p.m. Dutch people, men, women, and children were there. So they were to be interned, too? We stood or sat on the lawn; there was no shade and no protection whatever. As the sun rose higher we melted more.

At last there was action. Quite suddenly the men were separated from their families and marched away. We heard later they were taken to the Palembang jail, and there the poor souls lived. We have not seen them since.

Later the guards returned and marched us off—not to a ship and Singapore, but to a small street containing ten three-roomed cottages. We were told to go into these and *nanti nanti*—"wait". We are still waiting.

Most of these houses were stripped of furniture. There were twenty-four people in ours, seventeen sisters and seven other women. Next door were fifteen sisters and eight other people, including three children. This was good, apparently, for a slightly larger house farther along had thirty-six people in it.

We started from scratch. Taps but no water, electric lights but no power, small kitchen but no stove, no cooking pots, no wood, and still no beds. We had to eat something, so got a fire alight by removing a back door and smashing it to bits for wood. We borrowed a match from a guard to light the fire. We cooked in a shocking Mobiloil tin which had been half full of oil and spider-webs. We ate oiled rice and drank oiled tea for some weeks. The water and electricity were turned on, and so we settled in.

On to the floor we went again at night. No concrete, but cold tiles this time—certainly very cooling after a hot day. It is amazing how comfortable the floor can become! For pillows we used lifebelts or books or wood; some girls had tiny cushions. There was a cot in the bedroom, and as Sister James is only five feet high it was hers.

After a few weeks the wood question became acute all round the camp. We couldn't move any more doors. The top, sides, and back of our one and only wardrobe had gone, Sister James's cot was reduced to one tiny side piece, which she put on the floor at night to keep her off the tiles. Three rows of tiles were removed from the back of the house where the beams had to come down for firewood.

The wood situation was desperate. Dr Jean McDowell, our British spokesman, kept reporting to the guard-house just down the road and outside the barbed-wire barrier, asking for wood. Eventually they listened to her, for into that wood-hungry camp came one miserable-looking Japanese soldier, wheeling a miserable little lot of wood in a baby's pusher. He was surrounded by mobs of women and children until he didn't know where to put himself or his wood. They all talked at once to him, so he dropped it and went back for another little load. He was ridiculous! However, a little later a truck was driven into the camp, laden with wood—in fifteen-foot lengths and burnt black, but it was wood. The children were wildly excited and ran up and down the camp crying out, "Wood, plenty of it!" It kept coming, twice a day for days, and within a week we had so much wood we didn't know where to put it. It all had to be chopped, so two axes were provided for over four hundred women. They ran hot!

Rations arrived daily, and were thrown from a truck to the roadway. For weeks they were terrible. We could smell decayed vegetables and bad Chinese cabbages long before the truck bringing them arrived in the camp. Every now and then a piece of wild pig, called a "moving mass" by some bright soul, would arrive and be thrown on to the roadway, where it was immediately surrounded by dogs. We were not allowed to call the dogs away. The drill then was for a Japanese guard to cut it with his penknife into so many pieces—one piece to each house. He would put his dirty boot on the meat to steady it, since it was so tough, then he would throw each piece on a heap near by for us to take away when he said so. Our ration for twenty-four people would not cover the palm of a hand. Consequently there was great excitement if you found a small piece of pork in your stew.

Rotting long beans were also given to us. This green vege-table would have been good if there had been enough of it and some salt to add when cooking it.

Early in April we were suddenly awakened from our bore-dom by the arrival of two trucks full of women, children, and luggage. They had come from our old jail in Muntok.

We were hoping that more of our nurses would be with them, but no luck. They consisted mainly of British nurses and more civilians who had turned up after we left. Three came to live with us, Sisters Castle, Rossie, and McCallum. Some of us knew Mary McCallum, we had met her on leave at Frazer's Hill in Malaya before the war started.

We had heard rumours that Banka Island had been retaken by the British, but these people soon scotched that story. It is rather an amazing thing about camp rumours. Always something is about to happen a week or so ahead, but somehow it never comes off. It never fails to keep us interested.

After the arrival of these people the first rumour about being exchanged was started. Now, as I write this in October, the rumour still persists. All this is due to the fact that our camp personality Number One, who lived in Singapore before the war, has returned to camp after "being free" and not enjoying it! She tells us she has come back because we are all to be exchanged. We were also informed that her Chinese husband and children have already departed for Singapore. We wonder.

I am writing this spasmodically in a child's exercise book I was able to "obtain", but it is a very tricky business. We are not allowed to have papers or do any writing. Our belongings are searched periodically, without warning, and marriage certificates, birth certificates, or any personal papers at all are smartly removed and burnt by the guards. This diary lives in a small pillow at the moment.

One fine April morning we were rudely awakened by a Nipponese guard who told us we were to line up on the roadside at once for inspection by some high officials. This was before breakfast. We lined up in two rows. The guard inspected us, counted us, then told us very seriously, in Malay, that we were to bow low to the waist as the officials went past and we were *not* to laugh! I'll swear they don't know what next to expect of us. They wander in and out of our houses all day long with fixed bayonets—no doubt protection from so many females.

37

After this inspection the first people were freed from camp. They were Dutch Eurasians and Indo-Dutch. We don't know why they should be singled out, but good luck to them. A Dutch person told us that they had previously lived on vegetable plantations and tin-mines in the hills and were being sent back to work these places and improve the vegetable supply. Believe me, it needs improving.

We have had nothing but a small amount of what we call spinach, bringals, and long beans ever since we arrived, so little that when cooked together in a stew it amounts to a dessertspoonful per person. Every so often the rations don't come at all, so we eat straight rice without salt until the day comes when they do arrive. For months we didn't sight soap, then one day it arrived with the rations—a small piece each, which was treated like gold. Once we washed our few belongings with it, it was gone.

In May rations improved, and we were given a variety of water-lily roots, pink, mauve, and white. We all hope none of us dies here; we hate to think what might spring up from our burial places! We were also given bamboo shoots. We had heard so much about this delicacy, but we find it is hard, tasteless, and covered with tiny hairs, and is just as hard after cooking for an hour or so as it was before. We are now getting bad leeks, too. We like these because they add quite a good flavour to our food and can be smelt cooking from all corners of the camp.

As time passed we settled down to a daily routine, dividing the cooking and housekeeping, and taking turns to be the district nurse. Some of us were making up songs of camp life and what to do with the rations, just to pass the time of day while doing kitchen chores. One song is worth repeating. It was written by Val Smith and Ray, two of the sisters living next door. We would sing this madly at concerts, usually on Saturday nights—concerts that began with ourselves only, but were gradually enlarged as the rest of the camp joined us.

We sang this to the tune of "The Quartermaster's Store":

We are P.O.W.s pouring out our woes,
On a dreadful diet, this is how it goes:

There is rice, rice, mouldy rotten rice,
Nothing more, nothing more;
There are eggs, eggs, growing little legs,
Let's throw them at their shaven heads.

Chorus:
　　They are so blind they cannot see
　　This is not enough for you and me,
　　And we are all so damned hungry!

There is spinach, spinach, how the grubs thrive in it,
Nothing more, nothing more;
There are spuds, spuds, most of them are duds,
Let's throw them at these yellow thugs.

There is pork, pork, a skinny bit of pork,
Nothing more, nothing more;
There is yak, yak, yak we cannot hack,
Let's throw this tough stuff back.

There are leeks, leeks, oh gee, how it reeks!
Nothing more, nothing more;
There is cabbage, cabbage, rescued from the garbage,
Only good enough for yellow baggage.

Chorus:
　　They are so blind they do not know
　　How tired of this we all do grow,
　　And we all want to go home right now.

We are making quite interesting meals with rice, grinding
it and having porridge. Sometimes we would brown it and
offer the girls for their breakfast "ground brown porridge".
We have also made what we call cakes, pastry, and puddings.

On 14th May, my birthday, I was given a surprise party,
and surprise it was, too. We had a progressive bridge party.
For weeks we had been busy making packs of cards from
snaps we had removed from a Dutch photograph album we
found on a rubbish heap. We borrowed pens and red and
blue ink from some Dutch friends, and got busy. The results

39

were really excellent. We played a lot of bridge to pass the time away. Iole and some of the girls from next door came to the party, also a few other Australians who lived in other parts of the camp. My birthday presents had to be seen to be believed. Maudie James, an English lass, gave me a tiny curled cucumber wrapped up in a tinier piece of red georgette, which, she informed me, was a handkerchief. This gift I found lying beside me on the tiles when I woke up. Somebody else gave me a small bouquet of flowers she had picked in the jungle alongside us and from the cemetery behind our house. Iole gave me an oil painting, covered with spiders and webs—Heaven knows where she found it. It was a painting of a padi field. As if we didn't have enough rice around us without wanting pictures of how the stuff grew! The webs made it an antique, I was told. However, it serves its purpose and makes an excellent tray on which to dry our rice.

The prize for the progressive bridge was a little man made of rice. He was perfect. Our cooks that day made him, Jennie Greer and Beryl Woodbridge.

These two girls turned on a wonderful afternoon tea, everything being made from rice. They borrowed plates and dishes from the Dutch members and made doilies from old picture books. A small card told us what was on each plate. There were "Parachute drop-scones", "Ack-ack puffs", "Palembang pastries", "Post-Singapore sandwiches", "Pre-freedom sandwiches", *and* a birthday cake beautifully decorated with flowers and wild fruit from the cemetery, which looked very like strawberries. Oh dear, strawberries! On top of the cake was "Australia" and "A Happy Birthday" made from cut-out coloured paper. I was made to cut it, but found it was only an upturned cake tin and was quite empty!

A few weeks later something was celebrated next door and Iole invited me to dinner. Nobody knew what we were celebrating. We all sat down to dinner in a true party manner. Sylvia Muir, a Queenslander, who was full of ideas on decorating and floral arrangements, made the dinner table look a picture. There was invisible lighting—nobody knows where it came from—more cemetery flowers, cut-out paper mats, and so on. Each person used her own makan bowl for food and her own spoon. The spoons were amazing. There were old Chinese tin things about three inches long, small and large teaspoons, and coffee spoons. Tasmanian Shirley Gardham managed with a long-handled mustard spoon—she only knew how to shape her mouth to navigate the food in. Another lass ate with a shoe-horn and did quite well, said she was used to it now.

Del, Sister Delforce, was frightened one night. Del is a girl who will stand no nonsense. A Queenslander, she is very capable and quiet and has a heart of gold. Of medium height, with flashing dark eyes and hair, she gets on with the job regardless, and has one of the finest Australian vocabularies I've heard for some time.

It happened like this. We were all lying on the tiled floor trying hard to sleep when a Japanese guard started tramping up and down outside our house. He then decided to lean through the open window and flash his torch on and off our faces until we were wide awake. He did it to Del, who had been asleep.

Del was furious, and called out to him, "Take that damned light away, or I'll knock your so-and-so, repeat, head off!"

To Del's horror and our amazement, he answered in perfect English, "You wouldn't do all that, would you?" and disappeared. This slightly unnerved us, since he was the first guard we had met who could even understand us—and we didn't know which one he was.

Towards the end of May the Japanese camp commandant, Mr Ask-what-you-like-you-won't-get-it Miachi, came into the camp with a large bundle of papers, looking very important. He was a handsome fellow—that is, for a Jap—and wore his hair as our men do. He also had a dashing moustache and a good supply of English. He lived in Singapore before the war, we were told. He would come into the camp frequently, always smiling, and ask if we wanted anything, but somehow what we asked for never came to light.

He gave these forms to the British and Dutch commandants. Later they were distributed throughout the whole camp. Information was wanted about ourselves—name, age, birthplace, mother's and father's names, place of living, latest occupation, wife's nationality and "born" place, cash, valuables, and other property. We were quite sure this was for exchange purposes, so we all sat down, taking turns with the only pen in the place, and filled the forms in. As we are still here now we are wondering what is was all about.

Maudie James had us in fits one day. She arrived at our house dressed as a bride, proper bridal gown, complete with flowing veil. Her footwear rather gave her away, for she had her ankles covered with bandages—she had a few tropical ulcers—and awful looking "trompers" on her. She received quite a shock when we all rushed her to try to get that veil. The mosquitoes were very bad at night and we didn't have any mosquito nets. She dropped her bouquet, made of spinach, and fled. None of her costume belonged to her and she had promised to return it all to the owner.

Our days are now organized properly—trust nurses! We work to a schedule. Every day we have a different cooking squad of three people who do all the cooking and washing up for the whole house. It is a long day of jolly hard slogging, since the cooks must be up by 6.30 a.m. Once "cooking day" is over we can relax for a few days before it comes round again. Cooking rice and oddments three times a day for twenty-four people and trying to ring the changes is some contract.

We also have "housekeepers", a squad of two each day. One gets the only tin hat we own full of water and an old rag and washes the tiled floor throughout the house. Her offsider scrapes and cleans the drain that runs alongside the house, by dragging a wide and heavy hoe, called a chungkal, along, and making an unholy din doing it—especially Rene Singleton. She revels in it and has us all screaming at her as she goes past. Same offsider also washes the front and back porches when she can get the tin-hat bucket. This person also collects the rations out in the street, which runs down the centre of the camp. Life is very full on our working days.

Washing up is sheer joy. Only one bowl and one teaspoon to each person, so it is soon done.

The tin hat makes an annoying bucket because it is so easily tipped over when one is crawling on all fours scrubbing the floor. Water is far too precious to be wasted like that. Already our taps have been turned off and we have to queue up at the last house in the camp, which happens to be at the foot of a mild hill, and get all our water requirements from their one and only tap.

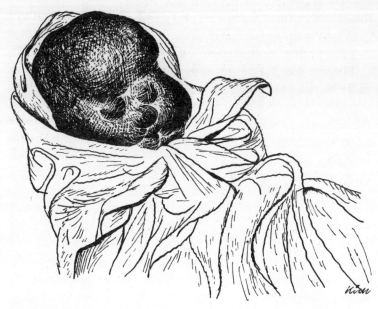

Chapter 8

EVERY Saturday night the sisters living next door give community singing concerts for all and sundry to air their lungs. These concerts have improved each week and now the variety of items could not be improved upon. The Dutch people have entered into the fun and games of it all and they sometimes give items in Dutch and English—songs, choruses, and so on. Some play the poor old battered piano which lives next door in House 7. Same piano is slept on every night—anything is warmer than tiles; Iole and Vivian sleep on a cupboard. Dutch Rita Wenning dances for us now and then; she dances beautifully. English Mrs Jennings, with a glorious voice, sings many songs; we make her sing "Little Silver Ring" more than others. Mrs Jennings also plays the piano well and cheers us up by playing everything we know so we can sing to our hearts' content. Miss Dryburgh, an English missionary, also plays accompaniments for the camp's best singers, Mrs Murray, Mrs Jennings, Mrs McLeod, and Mrs Chambers, who are all very generous with their glorious voices.

The last item of the evening is usually a bit of a shambles. We put on a play or some kind of skit on the various aspects of camp life. We have done "Ration Parade", "Palembang Paula Salon" with frocks *à la* concentration camp, and "Melbourne Cup", complete with horses, jockeys, and the radio announcer. We have also done "The Jolly Swagman" and "Riding Down From Bangor"—both absolute riots. We all go to bed exhausted on Saturday nights, we have sung and laughed too much.

Miss Margaret Dryburgh must have been in her late fifties when she was taken prisoner. She is English and had been in the East for many years as a missionary schoolteacher. She is very, very quiet and greatly admired by us all. She works hard for our entertainment, organizing church services every Sunday, running the glee club, and taking a hand in producing a camp magazine every month. This magazine has interesting articles written by people with us and includes a cookery section, a children's section, and even a crossword puzzle! In her own quiet way Miss Dryburgh is a very valuable member of the camp.

I asked Miss Dryburgh if I could copy two of her songs into my diary. Here is one, which we all sing to the tune of "Who Killed Cock Robin?":

All the folk in the camp stopped a-fretting and a-grieving
When they thought that Palembang they'd soon be leaving.

Who made the camp? We, said the Japs,
We're altering the maps, we made the camp.

Who lives in the camp? We, said internees,
Not long, if you please, we live in camp.

Who keeps them in? I, said the sentry,
I stand at the entry, I keep them in.

Who brings the food? I, said the lorry,
It's little, I'm sorry, I bring the food.

Who feeds the camp? I, said the rice,
Each day twice or thrice, I feed the camp.

Who makes rice nice? We, said the beans,
With eggs, yams and greens, we make rice nice.

Who cooks the food? I, said the fire,
A fan makes me higher, I cook the food.

Who brings the shop? I, said the bullock,
I climb up the hillock, I bring the shop.

Who chops the wood? I, said the axe,
I hurt many backs, I chop the wood.

Who digs the holes? I, said the chungkal,
I work in the jungle, I dig the holes.

Who heals the sick? The doctor said, I,
I've no great supply, I heal the sick.

Who helps the people? We, said the committee,
We need all your pity, we help the people.

Miss Dryburgh has also been busy writing "Alice in Internment Land", which is a gem. At the present time she is busy writing music in three parts for the "Camp Choral Society" or glee club. She writes from memory the music of well-known songs, so that each singer may sing from the music. Miss Dryburgh or Mrs Jennings conducts the singers and their efforts are really marvellous. How everybody enjoys it!

In a garage opposite us live fifteen English women, including Miss Dryburgh, all of them evacuees from Malaya or China or Singapore. Most of them are missionaries or mission teachers. Miss Livingston, also in her late fifties, is quite a personality in the camp. She is very tall and very thin, wears glasses and a white sun-helmet which is beginning to look as if it grows there. In the early days of camp life it was Miss Livingston who began to organize the food rations and wood supply. She still does and, thanks to her efforts, rations are not a bun-fight any more, but a well-organized routine.

Church service is held every Sunday morning in this garage

and is so well attended that we sit in the driveway and out to the fence. The missionaries take it in turns to take the service. A choir of five sing an anthem that Miss Dryburgh has written, and we all join in the hymns, which are written out for us on small scraps of paper.

On Sunday, 5th July 1942, we all sang "The Captive's Hymn" for the first time. Another, and the best, of Miss Dryburgh's efforts. We sing it at church every Sunday. Here are the words:

> Father, in captivity
> We would lift our prayer to Thee,
> Keep us ever in Thy love,
> Grant that daily we may prove
> Those who place their trust in Thee
> More than conquerors may be.
>
> Give us patience to endure,
> Keep our hearts serene and pure,
> Grant us courage, charity,
> Greater faith, humility,
> Readiness to own Thy will,
> Be we free, or captive still.
>
> For our country we would pray,
> In this hour be Thou her stay,
> Pride and selfishness forgive,
> Teach her by Thy laws to live,
> By Thy grace may all men see
> That true greatness comes from Thee.
>
> For our loved ones we would pray,
> Be their Guardian night and day,
> From all danger keep them free,
> Banish all anxiety.
> May they trust us to Thy care,
> Know that Thou our pains dost share.
>
> May the day of freedom dawn,
> Peace and Justice be reborn.
> Grant that nations, loving Thee,
> O'er the world may brothers be,
> Cleansed by suffering, know rebirth,
> See Thy Kingdom come on earth.

To hear people of all colours and creeds singing this each Sunday, is one of the things I shall never forget.

The members of this same garage amuse themselves by having charades and musical charades every so often. They are awfully good and we all dash over and look on. Mrs Brown, who must be in her sixties, gave an admirable performance one night as Dame Pêche Melba. We nearly died laughing at her. Some of them visited us in House 8 one night and did some acting. Where do they get their trappings from? They did a small play for us called "Citronella Ann". Ann was a sweet potato dressed in a baby's napkin and really looked like a baby. Said one member of the cast as she gazed into the bundle, "Oh, isn't she sweet?"

We had to do a play for them. Dorothy Freeman, Rene Singleton, Mickey Syer, and I turned on a scene from the midwifery section of a large public hospital. Apparently it amused everybody. Three anxious fathers sat in the "Visitor's Waiting Room". Mr Romano (Dot dressed as an Italian) was the hit of the night; Rene, in working clothes and her chung-kal, was poor nervous Mr Laceybottom worrying about his firstborn; and I was Mr Dionne. Mickey was the demented nurse trying to do her best for all concerned. It was quite fun.

Chapter 9

JUNE 1942 was a very important month, we thought at the time. We were all looking forward to our repatriation trip to India, via Singapore, according to strong rumour. As usual, it didn't eventuate. Later on the destination was changed and we were going to Lourenço Marques in Africa. We were to be exchanged through the Vatican.

> There are some young women who hope
> To travel by sea to the Pope,
> And there be exchanged
> As this good man arranged,
> So back to their homes and some soap!

As an antidote to our disappointment, Nippon made all arrangements to have the drains in the street cleaned by us—just to see us through the next six months, we thought. Our drains are just primitive open cuts in the earth, usually overgrown with tall grasses. The overflow from our septic tanks runs along these drains. After all, these small houses we live in were built for two or three people, not twenty-four. We are amazed at the Japanese idea of hygiene, and all this within a few miles of the Equator.

Talking of hygiene, the septic tanks are emptied every now and then by "Benjo"—a long, cylindrical affair on an old lorry, not unlike a petrol waggon. Benjo has the name "Neptun" inscribed on its sides. I often wonder how King Neptune would react if he knew. Accompanying this atrocity are half a dozen natives armed with large tins and they proceed to empty each tin from the septic tank into our open drain, which runs alongside the house and joins the main drain on the street.

When they weary of the job they rest on the ground *under* leaking Neptun and sleep for a while, or smoke a straw. Nobody has yet fathomed why they bring this thing into the camp when they hardly ever use it. While this work goes on one or two of the natives sit on their haunches and chew peculiar looking fruit while the "workers" are banging their tins round behind them. The smell is terrific! A cheery onlooker is the Jap guard with his pigstick. Why he doesn't swoon away is more than we can understand.

Our morale this month was no doubt elevated by the diet. For thirty days we had disintegrating cabbage, beans, and now and then one over-ripe duck egg between three people. We are getting filthy rice now, crawling with weevils and, as the Dutch say, "worrums". We also have to pick it over grain by grain to remove minute particles of broken glass, small stones, teeth, etc.

We play lots of bridge now. More cards have been made, the kings and queens being works of art. We play very seriously. Mrs Ward (English) has taught us contract bridge and we all love it. Veronica Clancy nearly drove us crazy at first with her "Clancy Convention", but we soon put a stop to that one! There is no doubt about it, bridge helps to make the weeks go by quickly.

One infuriating habit our "masters" have is counting, what

is called "tenko". We suddenly have to dump everything on the spot and stand outside on the roadway in the midday sun or rain and wait to be counted. Mitz, Sister Mittelheuser, a senior sister in our group, takes the bow. She has to stand at the top of the line and bow to the waist and say, *"Dua puloh umpat"* , which means "twenty-four" in Malay. We all mutter it individually just to help, and the guard, after counting half a dozen times, is usually surprised to find all correct.

In August we were allowed to have a "shop" in the camp. This shop was brought in by a rogue of a fellow called Gho Leng, who came into the camp on Sundays with a bullock cart of over-ripe pineapples, bananas, coconuts, limes, sugar, a minute amount of butter, tea, coffee, hard green peas like parrot food, weevily brown beans, and sandshoes. (Most of the British members of the camp were barefooted by this.) This was fine if you had any money.

Thank Heaven our diet improved! We were simply craving for sugar, for we had been given one ration only during this six months, and then only two pounds for the whole house. We were also longing for some fruit—the joy of having a whole banana to yourself! Pineapple, too, was wonderful after months of soggy rice.

At this stage Nippon apparently decided we weren't quite so frightening as he first thought, and Javanese police were sent to guard us—from what? Now, instead of rifle with fixed bayonet and slit eyes, we are guarded by one revolver, which last night shot a stray dog and wounded the poor thing. A few nights ago a Jap guard fired a shot from his rifle at a shadow in the camp very close to us and managed to kill outright another Jap! That's the spirit, boys! Makes one less for our chaps to polish off somewhere else. The fuss and *"susa"* the Japs made during the next twenty-four hours was most entertaining, though they had us scared stiff to move outside at night.

These Javanese "Policie" guards are dark-skinned natives and are a much more cheery object to gaze upon and be gazed upon by. They spend their days playing with the children of the camp, sleeping peacefully in the guard box while on duty, or de-lousing each other during our siesta hour.

September came, and so did Miachi. He again asked for ten nurses to go "free" and nurse at Pladjoe oilfields hospital. These large oilfields are across the river and only a few miles from Palembang. He sat on a fence opposite and waited for us to answer him. But he kept changing his mind. He wanted fifteen nurses. More nurses from all over the camp gathered —Miachi wanted twenty nurses. By four o'clock his mind was made up, he wanted thirty nurses. We were rather amused when he corrected an Australian accent he heard!

All nurses in the camp had a meeting to thrash the thing out. There were British, Dutch, Chinese nurses all sitting round on the floor, each one with plenty to say on the matter.

At 5 o'clock Miachi came back for his answer. Twenty or so people had volunteered half-heartedly, as the story was that we would be nursing two hundred American and Dutch men, and that they had asked for us. I bet they did! But nobody went free.

Some weeks later Miachi tried again and asked for more of us to nurse Japanese soldiers in their hospital. One or two said they would, but that, too, fell through. As a punishment we had three of our already packed houses taken from us.

We are now a community of four hundred women and children from all ends of the earth, living in fourteen small three-roomed houses and garages. The three houses we had to leave are still empty.

Three Dutch nurses couldn't bear this crowding, so went out to nurse in the Charitas Hospital in Palembang, about three miles from here. This hospital is run by Dutch nuns and doctors for all prisoners. It is only small and is an awful place. There is no ventilation in the wards at night; everything has to be closed because of mosquitoes and Japanese. I spent a week there after having an appendical attack, then begged to go back to camp in spite of having a wooden bench, a mattress and a pillow to sleep on. We were packed in that ward at night like sardines and we all hated it. The Allied servicemen, civilian men, and we women are all nursed here. We are separated into three divisions and are not allowed to get in touch with each other. The Japanese guard rather well between these wards, but do *not* guard the community lavatory. It is here we meet any Australian servicemen who happen to be walking patients, and they tell us the latest news. We haven't any radio in our camp now—all radios were smartly removed in the first few weeks—so this is the only way we can know what goes on in the outside world.

Women from our camp are taken to hospital on Wednesdays. One ex-British ambulance calls for us and the sick are bundled in. With them go those people with toothache or eye trouble—any excuse, really—so they can get to the hospital when they have had word that their husbands are there. The Japs pack as many as thirty-three of us into the ambulance, then a nightmare ride to the hospital would follow.

The sick are put to bed, the toothaches see the dentist (and their husbands), then the discharged patients, plus luggage, plus food bought on the black market, plus notes from husbands to wives—hidden, of course—with the toothaches and the eye troubles are returned to camp.

There is terrific excitement in camp when the ambulance returns. It is quite the event of the week. The children run up and down the camp, calling out, "Am-ba-lans!" and everybody hurries out to meet the home-comers and to hear the latest news.

As more people have been interned our crowded houses are nearly bursting. It never fails to amaze me to see as many as thirty people, all adult, streaming out from a tiny house for tenko each day. Four British sisters have left the crowded camp to nurse natives in a clinic in the town. They are working for two Dutch doctors, and have a small place to themselves to live in at night. They are apparently not worried by the Japs, from the few reports we have had of them.

This sleeping on hard cold tiles is beginning to get tiresome. We are gradually "acquiring" a rice sack each to put between us and the tiles. Some of us have stuffed them with grass. It makes the room smell like a stable, but it is a pleasure to go to bed now. Oh, for the day when we can sleep on a mattress, on a bed, between sheets, and not on a hard cold floor!

11th November 1942. Armistice Day. We had an impromptu service in our house conducted by Sister Jean Ashton and Mrs Jennings. We all wore our ragged uniforms with limp white collars, but as .we haven't any footwear we were barefooted. This service was a bit harrowing and I think we were all glad when it was over.

Jean Ashton is a South Australian and senior sister of the 13th A.G.H. girls next door. She is a tall, dark, very quiet and softly spoken girl who works like a slave. She is a marvel at keeping things under control. Life is not easy next door; there are some rather odd types living with our girls, and they are very hard to get on with, especially at ration time. Nobody is more honest than Jean Ashton.

14th November 1942. The British section of the camp went to a home-made polling booth today to vote for an official commandant. We all had a very amusing day, which resulted in Dr Jean McDowell being elected. Then we had to vote for a committee to assist her.

December 1942. I have been put on the "canteen committee", which consists of four British and four Dutch women, and is to cope with Gho Leng's shop that comes on Sundays. At last I have decided on my occupation when I get home—I'm going to be a wharfie and move cargo. I now spend the best part of the hottest mornings in the sun on Sunday, Monday, Tuesday, and sometimes Wednesday working with Mrs Jenkins. We unload all the heavy fruit and sacks of hard beans and other goods while a native sits by and watches. We then have to count everything and divide it equally for everybody in the camp. That takes about four hours. On Mondays Mrs Jenkins and I go back and divide out two tins of peanut oil into dozens of bottles for the camp. On Tuesday we sell anything that has been left over from Sunday. Wednesday, we tidy up the small store-room and have a committee meeting.

54

Chapter 10

Christmas, Camp Style

We were so sure we'd be home for Christmas that nobody gave it much thought, but December is going by and we are still very much here. O.K., we can take it, but what is next?

Presents for children and sweets for husbands, brothers, and friends in the jail—there was nothing else we could do for them. People had saved their precious gula, a type of sugar, brought in by Gho Leng for this. We also made presents for the servicemen.

We Australians got busy and in a matter of a few days turned a rafter from the roof into the snappiest mah-jongg set and sent it off to the Australian servicemen. During the making of that set there was no peace. Everyone put something into it. We sat on the floor and filed and filed with two old files we found, then smoothed each piece to a satin finish with leaves from a tree in the jungle near by. The backs of these leaves were like a fine emery paper. We then borrowed a set of paints from a Dutch nun and painted bamboos, characters, circles, winds, and flowers. It really was very good.

Other people in the camp have been very busy making quite useful things from old soempits—straw sack things that sometimes come with rations in them. They have made bags, purses, hats, slippers, and needle-cases. Dolls have been made, also handkerchiefs, from scraps of material, caps for the boys, belts made from rice sacks, games for the children (at the moment creating an unholy din in the street while the adult portion of the camp tries to siesta). Home-made snakes-and-ladders and ludo sets, a "Getting back to Singapore" game, and cards have also been made. Miss Moreton, who had been a teacher in Malaya, organized most of the presents. It was really a grand effort by all.

At Christmas time the camp choral society, consisting of both British and Dutch women, gathered on the veranda of House 2, where they were joined by almost everybody else in camp. This was the only spot in the camp where women could see their relatives in the distance each morning and evening. The men were building themselves a camp about a mile or so away. They were marched from the jail to this camp every morning and back each afternoon. On the way they passed this spot where we could see them; they were about four hundred yards away from us. Each time they passed they would stop and wave, then go on again. This day they waved and the women sang to them "Oh Come, All Ye Faithful". They stopped dead and listened, then, when we finished, waved hankies, shirts, and hats, and we heard an echo of, "Thank you!"

Two days later they stopped at the same corner and sang to us, the same hymn in English and then in Dutch. Everyone wept.

One afternoon the Dutch children did a small play of the Nativity and they looked sweet. They really looked like angels; the room was darkened and they did it by candle-light. Nobody knows where the candles came from or went to.

On Christmas morning there was a terribly long combined English and Dutch service at 6 a.m. Blanchie, Flo Trotter, and Senior Sister James were cooking squad for the day. They rose very early and had tea and *toast* (made from rice) ready for us before we took off for church. What stout fellows, it was a wonderful surprise. At church one of the missionaries gave us a short chat on how thirty years ago today she was saved from sin. We were fascinated, of course, and waited for more, but we didn't get it. All we learnt was that thirty years previously she was working in a Lancashire cotton mill.

At 9.30 a.m. there was another church service, English only this time, held at Garage 9 where the missionaries live. We sang many Christmas hymns and then listened to a long sermon. I think most of us would prefer more singing and less sermon at this stage.

At 11 a.m. we were "at home" and invited our friends to come along for morning tea. The cooks came to the fore and with the help of us all produced an amazing party tea. For once there seemed to be plenty to eat—we had been saving up for this. We had coffee and tea with *sugar*, even a hand-made cigarette to offer them afterwards. Chris Oxley and Jennie Greer made a small Christmas tree and decorated it, so things were not so bad at all, even in an internment camp. During the day the Japs brought in a typed paper of Christmas greetings from England, America, and Australia. Ours was signed by our Prime Minister, Mr Curtin, and read: "Australia sends greetings. Keep smiling. Curtin."

The British and Dutch men in the jail, who sometimes send us bananas hidden somewhere in the ration truck, which visits their camp before coming our way, sent us a huge tin of bully-beef, some coffee, and *soap*! We were thrilled. Later in the day pineapples arrived with a note: "This is to help have a decent meal on Christmas Day." The men's camp sent the women's camp a huge piece of beef, some tiny onions and potatoes—real potatoes, so that we could have one meal without eating rice and that foul vegetable weed stuff called "kang kong", which apparently thrives in the gutters and lakes around Palembang. What excitement to have a decent-sized piece of meat in the house! We all kept going to where the cooks were working just to have a look at it. The men can't realize just what a grand thing they did to the whole camp sending this food along. Goodness knows where they would get it from.

The Japanese effort towards our Christmas dinner had come to camp the day before. They sold us a duck-egg each, which we had for breakfast on Christmas morning.

For Christmas dinner we all sat at our table (Jennie's bed), the only piece of furniture, except for a sideboard, which was left in our house. We ate tender steak, fried onions, baked potatoes, and real gravy! These wonderful cooks also made a Christmas pudding from ground brown rice, peanuts, beans, cinnamon, and gula, which was a work of art and awfully good to eat. Chris made some potent drink she called chilli wine, which just about burnt our insides out. It was all topped off with a piece each of coconut ice given to us by three Dutch women from House 14.

The sisters from next door made and gave us a kangaroo, complete with joey in its pouch, made from a piece of old khaki shirt and stuffed. It is a beauty and is now our mascot.

In the afternoon there was a party in one of the Dutch houses for the children. There was a large tree there laden with presents, one for each child. They were thrilled with the toys and dolls they received.

28th December 1942. We have a Canadian, Mrs Layland, living with us here in House 8. She is a large person, most amusing and full of bright chat all day. We all like her very much. But last night she got the shock of her life. All the members of the household were asleep on the tiled floor when Mrs Layland was awakened by something moving under her pillow. To her horror she discovered it was a long snake and let forth a terrific scream. A guard came running, and she made him kill it. He informed her that she would have died in twenty minutes if it had bitten her. We teased her the following morning for screaming, and she told us she was "not a screaming female". Today she borrowed Jennie's eyebrow pluckers so that she could see the New Year in. Evidently her morale is restored!

A Dutch woman and her four children, the eldest aged seven, have joined us. They arrived with lots of luggage, each child carrying his or her own pack. They had been free all this time, miles away in the country somewhere, and had had a wireless, so proceeded to tell the news. It was simply "fighting in Malaya". That seems rather hard to believe.

Still more people have arrived—true kampong Malays this time, and black as your boot. Three are women, one about to have an infant, and four are children. All of them are lousy with scabies and fleas. As we are in one of the smallest houses with only twenty-four people already living in it, we were presented with these people and had to find a spot of room for them. We are now thirty-one in a three-roomed house. Heaven help us!

We got to work and cleaned out our kitchen and put the Malays and their fleas to live in there. They don't seem to mind much, and they have turned the backyard into a kampong. They squat round all day in a ring and cook queer-looking food over a brazier. Old Omah, the grandmother, and two of these small children do most of the cooking. They cut their vegetables on bricks in preference to the sink, peeling things away from themselves, exactly the opposite to our way of doing it. They spend the day spitting and spending a penny into the drain we work so hard to keep clean. They call each one of us "*Australie Mevrouw*".

Their news, which was the same as that given to us by other new-comers, startled us. It was that Singapore had been retaken by Americans and Chinese, held for three days only, then lost again. After that there was renewed fighting in Malaya and we held it as far as Penang. Also some excellent news—England hasn't been bombed for ten weeks.

The rumour spread and spread and was exaggerated so much that it eventually came back to us as, "Malaya and Singapore are in our hands, and it's only a matter of days before the Americans are here." Pack up, girls! The next thing was that somebody came home from hospital with the latest news—"Heavy fighting in New Guinea." Oh dear, did we come to earth! Today's news flash came in with the rubbish man—"The Americans are twenty-five miles away." So they might be, but I bet they are interned. Apparently these Americans are advancing fifty miles a day; we expected them at lunch-time, but it is now 5 p.m. and there is no sign of them. Mrs Layland is sniffing just outside the front door for them, swears she can smell pork and beans, and intends being the first to welcome them.

The rumours we have heard since last March are amazing. We all take them the same way—listen with much interest and pass it on, but nobody really believes it if it is too fantastic. However, one day we must get away, if we are patient.

An Indian called Milwani comes to the main guard-house, about three hundred yards down the road outside the camp barrier of barbed wire, and sells us poor materials, cottons and shoe-cum-slipper things, and other oddments at terrific prices. These can be bought only by those blest with money. Shipwrecks are not in the race. Being on the canteen committee, my job is policeman and I have to control the traffic as it were, and allow two women only at a time to go through the barrier. This is Nippon's order, so it must be done.

Last Wednesday it was far too hot for me to stand in the sun for two hours, so I sat on a box in the tiny guard's shelter just inside the entrance to our camp. The Javanese guard was lounging against a pole on the other side of the street and I hoped he would stay there. Then some busy soul started another rumour flying round the camp—"The Australians have taken Palembang." Great excitement until someone asked how did they know. It all boiled down to one fact: "There is an Australian sitting in the guard's shelter right now, go and look." How women do talk!

30th December 1942. No water all day. That is the latest idea our Nipponese masters have thought up, and it is not funny. As a matter of fact, there was a slight trickle late in the afternoon in House 14 at the foot of the camp, and a long weary queue of women and children waited patiently for hours to get some.

Chapter 11

January 1943. New Year's Eve was celebrated very differently this year, and rather quietly. There was nothing to celebrate. We all gathered next door to see out the worst year every one of us had ever put in, and hoped a decent new one would come in. We thought it would be hard to keep awake, since we are usually in bed by 9 p.m., but actually it was easy. Some of us were invited to a party over in Garage 9; Miss Glasgow was hostess, and we had a terribly funny evening, playing some hunting game which is the noisiest I've ever known. Rene Singleton was in her element representing a rooster; we simply had to shut her up in the end as the guard came along and snorted something at us.

After this party we went next door and joined the other Australian girls and played another amusing game organized by Jean Ashton. Just before midnight we had supper, then twelve o'clock came and went. We sang "Auld Lang Syne",

wished each other a happier New Year, then went home to
bed. Vivian and another lass found a tin of paint and made
menaces of themselves for a while before they, too, went
home to bed.

The men in the jail again sent us meat, onions, and
potatoes for New Year's dinner, so we all fared well once
more. It is a great comfort to know those men are there not
so far away.

We are having clothing trouble. Our shorts are still quite
whole, but sun-tops are wearing out very fast. We made
them originally from curtains, or lamp-shades, or old rags
thrown on a rubbish heap. However, we manage to look fairly
respectable and always lie on our folded shorts at night to
keep a crease in them. We should welcome a little money so
we could buy material from Milwani. We'll have to earn some
somehow.

A couple of days ago we were told to cut the long grass
in the camp in front of our houses. We had only a knife
without a handle to do this, and the cooks wanted the knife,
so it was all very awkward. We had to tidy up the grounds—
wood-heaps, fire-places, and all. The "Gun Sai Boo" ("say
boo" is right!) was visiting the camp for inspection. He,
apparently, is a big shot from "Syonanto"—we are not allowed
to say Singapore.

Word was quickly sent round the camp, "Don't wear sun-
tops"—which, of course, counted us out, since that is all we
have save our precious uniforms. We are keeping them to
wear home. So we wore sun-tops.

The guard had everybody sweeping the road at ten-minute
intervals for twenty-four hours before the big day. "Lipstick Larry" was on duty and he was in his usual foul temper.
He is a snitchy devil. He raced about the place all day like
a lunatic, shouting at us all until we were nearly at screaming
point. He is called Lipstick Larry because he can't bear the
sight of lipstick. A few Dutch women use it when they put
on a frock and a snappy hair-do in the afternoons. They stand
at tenko like this, a joy to look upon in these dreary surround-

ings, and along slouches this fellow and goes completely haywire at the sight of the lipstick, usually giving the wearer of
it a smashing blow across the mouth before fuming on his
bad-tempered way.

While all the road-sweeping was going on Iole was sitting
on a log in the garden over the way, innocently talking to an
Englishwoman, when she was suddenly attacked by Lipstick
Larry. Completely out of the blue, he raced yelling up to
her, armed with his rifle, stopped, picked up a wooden spoon,
and attacked her. From here it looked as if he were hitting her
quite hard, but actually, Iole said, he kept missing her. The
thought of being hit with a wooden spoon amused her so
much that she laughed at him. He was furious, so she got up
and ran for her life. He chased her, but it all ended happily;
Iole dodged him.

The next day the road-sweeping started again. It was the
big day. We swept and cleaned drains until we were wrecks.

Then the rations arrived. The natives on the truck in their
usual style threw the vegetables, bad bringals and smelling
towgay, on the beautifully cleaned roadway just inside the
camp entrance, then drove off smartly, leaving this untidy
mess smelling to high heaven. Before anything could be
done about it we heard a flourish of snooty car horns and
into the camp drove the "Gun Sai Boo" and his offsiders.
They deposited themselves within a couple of yards of this
offensive stuff on the roadway and stared at our rations. Five
men stood there for some minutes before our English and
Dutch commandants arrived and stood on the other side of
the rations. After fully fifteen minutes the men advanced and
they all got into a huddle on the roadway there and all seemed
to be asking questions at the same time. The "Gun Sai Boo"
took a quick glance at the rest of the camp from where he
stood, then got into his car and drove off. Result? Nothing
at all, as you were.

Next event to keep us from being bored stiff was the
Battle of the Bedroom next door. Poor Jean Ashton, trying
to keep the peace between her family of nurses and a wild

Irish family living there with them! It was all caused because a Dutch family was to live there when they arrived in camp. Everybody had been asked to move over and make room for five more in an already impossibly overcrowded house. There were ructions for a couple of days, then, as nobody arrived, peace reigned. The Irish wanted to keep changing their room, so eventually it was arranged that all we sisters should live together in one house. The other people in our place were quite happy to go and live next door, so it was a good arrangement all round. The only reason we had not lived together all along was because we thought it impossible for thirty-two to live in a three-roomed house—but it isn't.

Another nasty incident has cleared itself up. There is a tall Javanese guard we see now and then who always wears dark glasses, so he is known as "Fifth Columnist" by us all. But he has turned out trumps. He intercepted a letter written by a pro-Japanese member of the camp to ask for the removal of the Australian sisters to the padi fields. This letter got as far as the guard-house outside the camp where the Jap in charge asked Fifth Columnist to translate. He told the Jap that the camp people were complaining that the rubbish was not being removed often enough. While the Jap was away doing his round of the camp Fifth Columnist got hold of the letter and hid it on himself. During his next tour of duty with us he gave it to a Dutch woman who had employed him before the war. This woman was a friend of ours and handed the letter to us. We very quickly destroyed it. We heard later that the Javanese fellow spent some time helping the Jap search for the letter in the guard-house, with the Jap blaming himself for his carelessness!

Chapter 12

February 1943. There was great excitment at the beginning of this month and the best thing that has happened to us since we were taken prisoner. During siesta a few days ago Sister James was asked to go to House 14, where Mrs Muller lived, because a Japanese officer was there and had sent for her. Mrs Muller is a young Dutch woman with two small daughters, and is the only person in the camp who can speak Japanese. She had lived in Tokyo at the Dutch Embassy for some time before the war.

We all felt the worst was about to happen and anxiously awaited Sister James's return, thinking we probably had to go out and nurse Japs, but for once it was good news.

The officer was most interested in the Australian sisters, but kept calling them by a word that sounded like "kanka-foo"—apparently Japanese for "nurse", but too like our "kan-garoo". He wanted a full list of our names to send home to

Australia. Think of it—prisoners for a year and our families haven't been informed. The devils!

The next day he came again and saw our house, was thoroughly disgusted with our mattresses of grass, the worn thin rice sacks and torn sarongs we slept on, and appeared to be genuinely shocked when he heard we had not had sugar, milk, soap in any decent quantity, paper, sanitary paper, butter, beds, mosquito nets, and so on, and that we had to buy what little fruit or sugar we did have. He made a note in his book and promised things would be improved for us. Then he told us that Australia knew we were here in Sumatra and had sent a Christmas message. He also said we could receive parcels and be allowed to write one letter of thirty words home. If only we could! I wish we knew for sure that the list of our names had gone home. The officer spoke to each one of us asking if we had been "drowned". Some said yes and some no. Heaven knows we've filled in at least twenty lists of our names, addresses, ages, religion, sex, etc., but we do know there was a small bonfire outside the Jap guard-house each night the lists were sent in.

Because of this visit rumours are in full force again. There is another move in the air, each story says we are going to a a different place, here are some of them:

1. The jail.
2. The Lunatic Asylum for the Australians, the rest of the camp members stay where they are.
3. Juliana Flats.
4. One huge building, maybe a hotel, for the whole camp.
5. A hill station, Lahat, one hundred miles away.
6. Australia. (We can't believe that one.)

We have also been told we may take all our belongings, but not any pianos or refrigerators! So Flo Trotter at once got busy and painted "A.A.N.S." on our few belongings with what was left over of Vivian's paint.

Some of us are now earning our own living within the camp so we can buy sugar, fruit, and other things from Gho

Leng and perhaps save enough to buy material from Milwani to make night attire. The girls will do anything; some of them are chopping wood for people or doing their washing, minding their children, mending their trompers (if they have any), or cooking for families. After practising on the girls here I've developed into the camp barber at ten cents a trim, people providing their own scissors, which are usually curved nail scissors! The boys with their short hair I find hardest to trim.

Sewing scraps together to make something is the order of the day. We have one needle and there is almost a roster for it. We have also only one watch left that still goes. This precious article belongs to Jess Doyle and her patience is wonderful. At all hours of the day somebody pops her head in and says, "Could you tell me the time, please, Jess?" And no matter what that girl is doing, she answers at once, even if it happens three times in five minutes. We often wonder why we worry about time, but suppose it is just one of those survivals of a civilized life. We also keep a strict check on the date and day of the week, even if every day is the same. We have not any calenders, because the only one we had had a few stamps plastered on it picturing Mr Winston Churchill in a characteristic attitude. The Japs fairly tore them off when they saw them, and the calender was ruined.

We are always busy with the needle, making blouses, pillows, work-bags, towels, and tea-towels from scraps. Iole and I had been very busy making a mosquito net. It belonged to Iole at first and was made from the back half of the skirt of a black net evening frock. It was large enough only for her head. Now we have added the remains of Win's old sarong, an old skirt picked up somewhere, the remains of my only voile frock, affectionately known as "Miss Livingston" because that good lady gave it to me early on, and now we have a colourful and large net. We can both get under it and get some peace from these endless mosquitoes. It hangs from anything hangable within reach of our particular area of floor, called our bed-space, and is known to us all as "Rule Britannia." It is a grand old net.

68

We are all more or less protected from mosquitoes in this way now, and anybody trying to walk through the room after 9 p.m. is likely to get caught up in the maze. After all, we are all lying on the floor shoulder to shoulder with our bed-space rationed to two and a half tiles per person.

28th February 1943. Our toothbrush troubles have caught up with us. At first we had one, which was shared. The user washed it and dried it in the sun before the next one used it. Then we were given a few more by the Dutch women before they were interned. Now they are worn out and our tooth-ache is starting. A classic remark from Flo Trotter in the "bathroom" last night was, "My teeth are almost too sore to clean these days." Fillings have fallen out and we cannot get any dental treatment any more at the hospital. We shall all go home toothless and white-haired if the Russians don't come soon. Seeing that the Americans didn't arrive, for some extraordinary reason, rumour now hath it that the Russians are on the way. I don't know how this story started unless it is because of Mischa, a four-year-old Russian boy with us, who lost his parents on the *Vyner Brooke.* Every time the rations come he rushes out on to the roadway and calls out, "The Russians, the Russians!"

9th March 1943. Del and Blanchie have just completed a beautiful mah-jongg set and have decided to sell it to buy food and clothing. Five sets have now been made by different girls, so we are getting quite adept at it. Some of us have been given orders for more mah-jongg sets, and for dominoes and chess sets. They take a long time to make.

Rations have been cut again. Today we were given six baby cucumbers, soft and oozing, six bunches of kang kong and four soft bringals for thirty-three of us. We are going to be hungry again tonight.

There was a house captains' meeting held last night; the subject rather tickled us and we sent our Mitz along with strict instructions to tell us everything when she came back. Subject was, "What is to be done with the bitch in House 1?" The funny part is that they were deadly serious.

11th March 1943. I hate this damned hole! When ever will the day of freedom come? It's terribly hot and the water is still turned off. We would give anything to know what is going on in the world outside the barbed wire. We were given one bunch of leeks for the whole camp today and half what we were given yesterday.

We have all decided to be drooping lilies when we get out of here; we are learning fast from observation.

13th March 1943. Red letter day! At last P.O.W. postcards have actually been given to us to write to any part of the world in English, Malay, or Dutch. After about six months of talk about these things they have at last come to light. Now the question is, what do we say? We have been given strict instructions on what we are *not* to write; seems a pity as there is so much to say. However, as long as they get home with our own signatures that our families will know we shall all be quite happy.

We were also all given an anti-dysenteric injection today. What has bitten the Japs?

15th March 1943. My father's and Iole's birthdays today. Iole had a good day, much better than last year when the notorious Japanese officers' club was in full swing. Small vases of flowers arrived for her all the morning. In the afternoon we had another bridge and mah-jongg party. More prizes of rice novelties.

The P.O.W. letters were collected this morning and, we hope, have gone on their way.

18th March 1943. No water now for four days; even House 14 has been cut off. We have to go outside the camp and down the hill to the guard-house, *when* he says so, and carry it back up the hill.

We are beginning to get typhoid in the camp now, and already one woman has been sent to hospital with typhus. It wasn't a Wednesday, ambulance day, either. Dr McDowell used her influence with the Japs and it frightened them so much that an ambulance was sent at once.

Even coping with typhoid under these conditions is quite

grim. We are now doing day and night duty and madly digging holes in the jungle alongside us to empty bedpans; there is no other way in which we can avoid spreading infection. Houses are too overcrowded.

Birthdays are coming thick and fast, Blanchie's today. She refuses to tell us how old she is, says she is not counting the two she has had here. This dark-haired, dark-eyed girl from the Northern Rivers district of New South Wales is a most amusing and likeable soul. She was a wizard at her job in the operating theatre in Malacca and Singapore. I shall never forget seeing how calm she was while we were being shelled one morning in Singapore. She refused to stop working and more or less made everybody round her feel quite calm, too, and that to get on with the job was the thing. However, we gave her a birthday party, and with the help of fruit from Gho Leng made it a fruit-salad tea party. Beryl Woodbridge made and gave Blanchie a beautiful Balinese dancing-girl doll. Nice work, Woodie.

19th March 1943. We have decided to put all books found in camp into a communal library so they can circulate more freely. It works out at one book to three people, which is a much better average than before. Some rather good books have come to light.

More Dutch people have arrived today, two women and five more children, plus all their belongings. The children had knapsacks tied all over them, one being made from a flour-bag on which had "Made in Australia" printed all over it. Oh dear, so near and yet so far from home!

We have been here for thirteen months, and if somebody would send a plane, we could all be in Darwin in a day's time, safe and sound before anything more should happen to us.

Chapter 13

1st April 1943. It is a year ago today since we were rudely awakened by that Jap guard and told to be ready to move and in the padang in half an hour. Instead of being taken for the anticipated trip to Singapore, we were told to shelter from the sun in this house. At first it was for a few hours, then for one night, then for forty nights. We are still sheltering. Have they forgotten to come for us? We haven't given up hope yet, but if we are still here next April Fool's Day we won't be worth saving. We are growing into very snitchy beings.

I have just been told rather a fantastic story by a young Dutch mother who was recently brought into camp with her family of children. She didn't know how to get her money in without the Japs finding it, so she made a rag doll for her six-year-old daughter and stuffed it with hundreds of paper guilders. The only instructions she gave the child were to look after the doll herself as it was her very own, and not to allow anyone, particularly a Japanese, to take it from her. During a three-day journey into camp not once did that child allow the doll to be taken from her arms. She did not know about the money; she just knew it was very important.

We have started having air-raid practice. This sounds hopeful. The A.R.P. wardens are Javanese boys of about eighteen years who dash about the camp with sticks about six feet long and crowd us all into two houses, two hundred to a house—it's wicked.

We have an addition to our house. Dorothy Freeman and Rene Singleton have built themselves a "flat". It is literally hacked out of the jungle alongside us. Iole and I helped them to move the barbed-wire barrier out a few feet, which has not yet been discovered by Nippon, and a crude shelter has been attached to the trees forming a roof. A table and old sink Dot found in the cemetery have been added and there they cook. Every Thursday seven of us gather here and have what we call a discussion group, five Australians and two Dutch girls, Helen and Antoinette Colijn. So far we have had Helen working overtime; she can get at the Dutch literature in the camp and translate for us. She has already translated *Madame Curie* for us and given us many interesting facts of Dutch history, covering both Holland and the N.E.I. We have played fair and told them quite a lot about our country. We have geography and general knowledge quizzes, discussing thoroughly anything we don't agree on. This is all to keep our brains from rusting and really has a good effect on us.

The best news of the day is that the men have asked the Japs if they can cut our wood, so cut wood now arrives in the camp. What a tremendous relief this is! We have had some bad accidents with the old blunt axe whose head flies off once every five minutes. It is also another way of getting notes from the men to their wives. Every now and then somebody finds a note tucked away in a piece of split wood, which causes much excitement.

It is terribly hot; day and night we seem to be stifling; there is no water whatever, we are still carrying it from the guard-house for cooking, bathroom, washing, and lavatory. The only time we can get clean is when it rains, then we all drop everything and go outside and stand under the largest leaks coming from the roof and wash our hair and ourselves to our hearts content.

8th April 1943. Rice has been reduced to one cigarette tin per person per day.

Some Dutchmen in the men's camp have sent us sisters three live fowls. We have had more fun with those fowls than anything for some time. I couldn't possibly describe a Palembang fowl except that it has long thin legs and a high thin body. We had great arguments, are they hens or roosters? We waited for a day to see if any eggs would appear on the scene, and as we had the fowls tied by a leg to an old bush in the back yard we should soon have found them if there had been any. During siesta one cock-a-doodle-dooed, and the rush to see which one did it was terrific. One rooster. For another day we waited wondering which was what, then old Omah, the Malay grandmother from next door, tottered in, all smiles, took one look at the birds and said, *"Ya, ya,* sister, *tiga laki laki"*, which literally means "three husbands". So we decided to eat them. Mavis Hannah and Elizabeth Simons set to work to kill them. The axe was so blunt that after the first whack the poor brutes were not separated from their heads. However, the first two heads eventually came away, but not so the third. Its owner got away from us and flew up on the roof. After much chasing it came down—it apparently couldn't bear the strain—and into the oil-tin it went to be cooked. We had one glorious meal of chicken, quite a goodly portion each, and two lots of chicken broth, in spite of three thin fowls between thirty-three hungry women.

Sunday, 11th April 1943. Big news! We were told today of the future existence of yet another camp for the married people. "Family internment" is the term being used. It will remove many Dutch families from our camp and their husbands, brothers, and sons from the men's camp.

Item number two this day was the immediate transfer of the

biggest boys to the men's camp, as there is not enough room here for big boys. One lad is over six feet, though he is only twelve, and had to live with his mother, three sisters, and young brother in one tiny room. Nine boys left us; we shall miss them, since most of them have been a great help to the camp generally as well as to their mothers.

On Thursday evenings the camp gathers outside House 5 where the British commandant lives and we listen to half-hourly talks given by different members of the camp. A missionary, Miss Prowse, gave us a very interesting chat about the stars; Dr McDowell told us about Palestine; our Shirley Gardham spoke of Tasmania; Mrs Maddams (English) told us all about a Malayan rubber plantation, and Mrs Gilmour about life on a leper station. Among other subjects were "Working in a Cotton Mill", "Life of a London Manne-quin", "Behind the Footlights on a London Stage", "Life of Chopin", and "Life of Rudyard Kipling". We were told by a Dutch lass that in Holland in winter it was rather fun to take a train from The Hague to Amsterdam, one hour's trip, and skate home again along ice-bound canals—how absolutely super!

Saturday, 17th April 1943. Who has won a battle lately? Today when we went out for tenko the Jap guard, "Banana Johnnie", *saluted* us both coming and going—absolutely unheard of! All the same, we haven't had our once-weekly meat bones for some time.

Tonight we had some fun and put on an act for the camp, our ideas on what family internment should be like. We've rocked them all! I don't think they are so keen.

25th April 1943. Anzac Day, remembered for the first time in Palembang. We had a service for all Australians in camp at our house; the choir came, too, and helped us. We found this service very hard to take.

26th April 1943. Easter Monday, so the missionaries tell us. We thirty-two had a bridge party this morning, with tiny scorers drawn by Vivian, Del, and myself. We drew a chicken hopping out of an egg with an air-mail single ticket to Australia in its beak. *That* will be the day! It was Del's idea about the chicken.

There was a concert given by the camp choral society this afternoon; they sang beautifully old English, Scottish, and Irish songs and finished up with the whole camp singing "Jerusalem". It sounded marvellous. Some of the more energetic people did folk dances and old English country dances outside on the roadway in the hot sun.

29th April 1943. Jap Emperor's birthday, we shall probably get a few bad duck-eggs in the rations as a "present". No hundred guns boomed forth as they did last year.

A "young people's club" has come into existence for those girls who are missing the best school years in their lives, and some of us are asked to help arrange competitions, games, and so on on Friday nights. We entertained them here last week with charades and at their request put on an operation scene in shadow, which was rather fun and brought the house down. The roars of laughter brought a couple of Japs along with their rifles; they thoroughly enjoyed themselves. We borrowed a sheet and arranged the light behind it and the actors. Wonderful effect!

May 1943. Who would believe it? We're still here. When *do* we leave this awful dump? We are used to not having any water, but now they have stopped the tiny bit of sugar we were getting. This has been replaced by seven soempits of what looks like decayed cow's horns, but has turned out to be dried tapioca root, which is absolutely filthy, full of mildew and dirt, and quite tasteless. However, when washed, dried, and pounded into some semblance of flour, this is food and helps us on our way. The children had quite good fun with it at first and used it for chalk, the camp road being now covered with drawings. We are told the correct name for this is *gaplek*. Odd, dirty, hard little yellow beans came, too, hard as the hobs of hell. These are called soya beans and are terribly bitter.

12th May 1943. Jap guard of a nastier type than usual came into camp today and asked for Mrs Layland's clothes because she was going free. This was staggering news, for we knew she was very ill in the hospital in Palembang. Everything was bundled up and taken to the guard-house. A little later we heard Mrs Layland had died in hospital. She had asked the Japs to give all her belongings to an internee friend, Mrs James. Mrs James was given what Mr Jap didn't need for himself. Nice types, the Japanese.

20th May 1943. A Dutch nun, Sister Paulie, the prettiest and fairest nun of all here in camp, is now giving us drawing lessons. We are able to buy some paper from Milwani, so we can draw and learn to paint with this small tin of children's paints owned by Sister Paulie. So far results are quite promising. Pat Gunther is quite good at painting, looks like a hidden talent coming to the fore.

Miachi, Mr Ask-what-you-like-you-won't-get-it, has left us long since and our new boss, Kato, took himself off to Singapore on our behalf, so he told us. We at least expect a letter, or a parcel, or repatriation or something, but so far nothing has happened and we're so tired of sleeping on this cold tiled floor.

A German woman who has been in camp with us was given her freedom and now works for Jap officers at the ex-Burgemeester's house as housekeeper-overseer. What a title!

Speaking of overseers, Iole gave a very interesting talk on life on an Australian sheep station last Thursday night. She nearly drove us all crazy for a week beforehand while getting it together; there are quite a few of our girls here whose families are on the land at home. A while ago Shortie, a Queenslander, gave the camp a talk about cattle stations, which had some rather amusing incidents when question time came. One person asked her how much milk they got from the cattle and what did they do with it all.

Those awful little hard beans and dried cow's horns are now arriving each Sunday. We had a new brand today which looked like grey cuttlefish—I ought to know as Dutch Joss and I have to ration it out to the camp. The beans give us colic and diarrhoea and the other stuff has the opposite effect, so we should have a well-balanced diet.

Mitz, today's cook, has just produced what she calls "curry puffs", filled with curried soya beans. They are good. Last time we had curry puffs was at the Malacca Swimming Club in 1941.

Iole and I have just finished a super mah-jongg set and sold it for eighteen guilders. Whacko! That will buy us some fruit from Gho Leng's dwindling supply on Sundays. He doesn't bring us sugar at all now, says he can't get any. The bright side of that story is that Australian sugar must still be Australian owned!

25th June 1943. Have had my diary sewn up in a small pillow for a few weeks because the boys have been searching amongst our few belongings again looking for Heaven knows what. Nothing much has happened except that Iole was suddenly whisked away last week to hospital. I expected her back yesterday, so I mended and washed her shorts and sun-top, and borrowed the only iron in the camp to iron them, but she didn't come back. She is alright, apparently, and staying for another week for observation.

Kong, a Chinese nurse from Singapore, who is here with us and doing a wonderful job nursing in the camp, gave us an amusing talk last night on Chinese customs and humour. She had us in fits of laughter for an hour, telling us about old Chinese remedies, such as pounded cockroaches for fever and paste made from tiger's nails for mumps. She uses the least number of English words she possibly can, leaving us madly filling in the spaces to get the hang of what she is saying. She knows the words well enough, but can't be bothered using them.

To finish off her talk, she told us of a Chinese custom in which a parent is mourned for fifteen years after death, then the grave is opened and the bones therein are washed with brandy, then reburied. After that there is no further responsibility. Kong had seen this done when her father's grave was opened.

Chapter 14

29th June 1943. We have decided to stop cooking in one large group and to try ourselves out in smaller groups of two or three. "Kongsi" is the camp word for small group. We are all beginning to get too tired, and cooking days are hell. We have just had a meeting on the bedroom floor to discuss this, so we begin in our small kongsis tomorrow. Heaven knows where we will get enough pots and tins from, we are desperate enough now.

30th June 1943. We are beginning to get a little worried about our girls. Iole is still in hospital and now Blanchie and Tweedie (Joyce Tweddell) have gone, too. Blanchie has a shockingly infected throat and Tweedie has dysentery. We can do so little for them here.

3rd July 1943. Beryl Woodbridge, known to us as Woodie, a small, dark, wavy-haired, pretty girl, who just bubbles with kindness and happiness, dashed into the house last night after visiting some English friends and wakened us from a dead sleep by saying that Germany had signed an armistice with England! She went very flat when little enthusiasm was shown; we can't believe that one yet. We often wonder how we will react when our day of freedom comes. Guess we won't believe it until we see it.

7th July 1943. Another sister went to hospital today, Flo Trotter. That makes four of our girls in there now.

Some black cotton material, yards of it, has been given to each house to make adequate black-out shades. We were so badly in need of material to replace worn-out shorts that we made very neat little black-out lamp shades, and quite a few neat little pairs of shorts! So far we have been able to get away with it and nobody is any the wiser.

Jap officers visited us today, then sent for all house captains to go to the guard-house. There they asked for another list of our names, etc. They must have at least three hundred by now. "Stand up, Australians," said one of the officers. Our Mitz stood up. He gave her some sheets of notepaper. "You make separate list," he said. He gave her still more paper. Mitz must have winning ways. We wonder what this list will bring forth?

The Jap guard we call "Heart of Gold" took the count that evening. He is a funny old thing, when he takes tenko he simply can't count and is usually quite drunk. Mitz, as captain, took the bow as usual, then he led her back from the roadway where we have to stand and round to the back of our house. He showed her a small hole in the hedge between us and the Chinese cemetery behind—a hole worn by dogs and Jap guards. Not our usual entry to the cemetery at all. "Heart of Gold" and Mitz then came back to the line, and, drunk as he was, he proceeded to tell us all in awful Malay not to go out though that hole to buy things from the native population. If we continued to do this—and, I might add, we never have done it—we would be shot and then have our faces smacked! We couldn't help laughing at this, and old "Heart of Gold" realized what he had said and burst out laughing, too, then staggered on his way.

7th September 1943. All the girls are back from hospital.

11th September 1943. Iole wakened last night and saw a native half inside the open window, bending over Blanchie and trying to remove her precious striped sheet. Nobody knows officially where the girl found this sheet, but there are quite a few in the hospital. We don't ask awkward questions these days. Iole called out, *"Pergi!"* and the fellow vanished. As Blanchie is deaf in one ear now and was sleeping on her good one, she didn't hear anything and slept serenely on, while Flo, Iole, and I wandered round in our scanty night attire in the bright moonlight to report the native to the Javanese guard. When we found him down in the street and called him over my two friends decided to leave me to it, dear souls, so I struggled alone with the story in my best Malay, then, realizing how futile it all was, left him and went inside, too. A minute later the guard put his head in the window and said, "Good night, girls." The cheeky devil!

What a day we have had today! Materials came for us, new coloured voile stuff, so thin you can see straight through it, but it is *clean*. This is very welcome since Milwani does not come any more. Bundles and bundles of this voile were brought in for all the women. We have been asking for it for eighteen months. As we have not had anything but men's cast-offs to wear we were given some bits and pieces to make night attire and panties. We decided to auction it by drawing cards. Mitz stood on our only piece of furniture and we drew cards for the mauve, the pink, and the blue. Least popular was the green and yellow striped—a shocker of a pattern. I kept drawing fives and threes, so eventually a five won me some of the green and yellow. I shall now proceed to bed in a knee-length nightie, looking like a tiger. All we want now is some cotton to make up the material. We use drawn threads from an old piece of sheet. We still have our one precious, rusty needle.

12th September 1943. More air-raid practice, and from now on a permanent black-out. That is good news. Today the whole camp had to move once more into two small houses during this practice. Two hundred of us in each house, and was it hot!

13th September 1943. Things are happening fast. Today buses pulled in down the road just outside the camp barrier and opposite the main guard-house, and deposited hospital nursing nuns and Dr Goldberg at an empty house there. Dr Goldberg was with us on the *Vyner Brooke* and has been in charge of the women's section of the hospital. She was not given any notice at all to be ready for this move. A little later more buses arrived from Palembang bringing our women patients, who soon settled in at this new hospital. We may visit our friends at certain times each day, we are told. Thank goodness the hospital is close if we are going to have air raids.

18th September 1943. The buzz of gossip and excitement in camp is terrific. All camps are moving, first the men from their camp about a mile away, then only the married men are going. Each hour the story changes: the men have gone, the men haven't gone. There has *never* been a better place for gossip than this spot where hundreds of women are crowded in together!

Finally some chopped wood from the men arrived in camp and some lass found a note tucked away in a piece of wood saying, "Leaving today—destination unknown." Later we saw them in the distance, leaving in trucks.

So ends our chopped wood, and we start fracturing our skulls once more, trying to cut spare parts from wrecks of ships with our blunt old axe.

Now we are moving, nobody knows where, somewhere between Guam and Africa. Somebody is bound to be right, even if we only go round that corner down the street outside that has intrigued us for so long.

Chapter 15

The next entry was written on a separate piece of paper in very small writing. As things got very willing and we were instructed to burn all papers, the diary was once again sewn into my small pillow, where it stayed for some months until things settled down again.

25th January 1944. Here we are in 1944 and still on the wrong side of an internment camp. It is two years since we saw the outside world and, oh, this place is so ghastly! We all loathe it more each week. This new camp is like a pigsty.

We were right way back in September. We did move that very day I finished my last notes. About six officers walked into our house and gave us one hour's notice to pack up. People from the first three houses only in the camp were to move that day. We were ready in ten minutes.

Later on a truck containing a few natives lumbered up the hill and stopped outside our place. The natives got out and rolled and smoked a straw while we packed that truck with our "furniture" and "luggage"—precious pots, tins, pieces of wood, and our bundles of rags, our clothes. In about ten minutes there was not one inch of room anywhere on that truck, the natives were open-mouthed; they had never seen such fast work. Three of us who were in the truck packing things as they were handed up to us had to stay there, because we were packed in, too. So we went with the truck. At the last moment Dot Freeman came running out with a wobbling pudding in a flower-pot, which she asked me to hold all the way, wherever we were going, as it was unpackable. Dear old Dot, we made it, that pudding and I.

The other members of the household followed in another truck, and that is how we went to the camp about a mile away, a filthy place built on a swamp, below sea level, and evacuated the day before by the civilian men. God, what filth!

The camp was a rectangular open space, about one hundred yards long, forty yards wide at one end and narrower at the other, and one tap! There are three empty wells, a blade or two or grass, and all surrounded by attap-roofed huts. Down the centre of each hut is a long mud or clay passage with a wooden shelf each side, two feet from the ground and about five feet six inches wide, on which we sleep. We are sixty to one hut, and lie alongside each other like sardines. Our belongings sit on a narrower shelf above our heads.

The Dutch live in the huts on one side of the camp and the British on the other; all seemed happy that way. At the far end are the British and Dutch kitchens. The opposite end is actually the entrance, with a guard-house in the middle, our hospital on one side, and about fifty Dutch nuns on the other. The outer walls of these huts form the barrier; they are boarded up to the roof and we can now see outside only through cracks in the boards.

The place is thick with bugs, rats, fleas, mosquitoes, and mud. For days we worked hard trying to clean it all up. The roof does not meet in the centre as it should, as it blows up with a "Sumatra", a violent gale, a couple of times a week and this lifts the palm-leafed roof, and in comes the rain and wets us through. It pours on to the clay passageway down the centre and leaves it absolutely treacherous. Already three of our sisters have developed malaria.

There are two bathrooms for the whole camp, which now holds over five hundred, since all free Dutch, Germans, and free "girl-friends" have been interned. One bathroom is on the Dutch side and one on ours. They have to be seen to be believed. As one Scots lass said, "I wouldn't put my cows in here", while another Scotswoman described the whole camp as "cattle pavilions at the Edinburgh Show".

Our bathroom is large and has a cracked cement floor, with a large cement trough, called a tong, in the middle. This is meant to store water for washing. There are two taps over it, but they haven't been used for months and are full of spiders, definitely no water in them. I should think those taps have never worked. However, that did not stop two bright girls who got up on the roof and tore away the attap over the tong, so that when it rains it catches water. When it is fine the sun streams in and keeps the floor dry and helps us to dry ourselves. There are very few towels amongst the British these days.

The lavatory is here, too, in the bathroom. It is a long cement drain, that is all. One needs to be a contortionist before becoming adept at it. The septic (?) tank by the drain outside has to be "done" daily by a Dutch girl and a Britisher. They go off to their foul job each day quite happily before breakfast. Their tools of trade consist of half a small tin on a stick and a kerosene tin.

The wells are filling a little now with the rains, but the mud and slush round the well-head is terrific. As nobody has a watertight tin to throw down there is water everywhere but in the proper place. However, this is precious water, for the one and only tap which can perform—when the Japs don't turn it off at the main outside—is not enough, and the queue of at least one hundred buckets never seems to lessen.

85

Of course we are having lots of accidents in the wells. Very early in the piece a young Dutch child fell while carrying a bucket of hot rice porridge, and it went all over his legs. His mother raced along, picked him up, and threw him in the nearest well. That was all right for helping the burns, apparently, but the next minute he was drowning in about four feet of water, so somebody else had to jump in to pull him out!

On another occasion, Rita, a Dutch girl, decided to jump into the deepest well to rescue precious water tins that had fallen in. It was easy getting in, but what fun getting her out! It was rather funny seeing these tins being thrown up and out of this well by Rita, and great excitement for the tins' owners, but the only ladder did not reach her. At last she got out with ropes and the ladder—said she quite enjoyed herself.

After three months in this mud swamp the Japs have built what we call a shelter shed, and the Dutch call a pendopo, right in the middle of the camp, in which the children play and scream their lungs out from 6 a.m. till 6 p.m. Church is held there on Sundays and school during the week. Missionaries and nuns take the school classes. On odd occasions we have a concert here, too.

Norah Chambers conducts her "orchestra" in the Dutch kitchen at night. There are no musical instruments. About twenty women of all nationalities hum or "ooh" very softly music that has been written down from memory by Miss Dryburgh and Norah—glorious music. I loved listening to them doing the Largo from the "New World" Symphony, and "Raindrop Prelude", but they are doing more and more each week. I have been a keen listener for a long time, but now I am a member of the orchestra. It is absolutely marvellous, the most fascinating thing I have ever done. We are doing the "Moonlight" Sonata, "Morning" from the *Peer Gynt Suite*, "Country Gardens", "Sea Song", "Bolero", and quite a few others.

The orchestra is divided into firsts, seconds, thirds, and fourths, and all practise during the day in their four separate groups. On practice nights they all come together and are conducted by Norah. This music is quite the most wonderful thing that has happened in this camp so far. None of us have ever heard women's voices anywhere better than this orchestra. The music is written out on any kind of paper obtainable; each person has her own copy, all being copied from Miss Dryburgh's hand-made original.

To sit on logs or stools or tables in the crude old attap-roofed kitchen, with only one light, and then to be lifted right out of that atmosphere with this music is sheer joy. It is so easy to forget one is a prisoner.

The first concert the orchestra gave they did the Largo, "Andante Cantabile", Mendelssohn's "Song Without Words", a Brahms Waltz, "Londonderry Air", Debussy's "Reverie", Beethoven's "Minuet", and "To a Wild Rose". Mrs Murray, with her glorious soprano voice, sang the Fairy Song from *The Immortal Hour*. It was a glorious concert, we had never heard anything like it before.

February 1944. Back to the diary again; it has survived another search.

We are allowed a daily shop now, still being brought in by a Chinese. I find I am still O.C. fruit for the British when it comes, and what a job! Trying to please everybody when bananas are big, little, green, bad, and only one each, is a foul job and a tiring one, too. Dutch Joss and I have to unload the bananas, carry them into camp, cut them into "hands", then count and grade them so each section of the camp gets the same mixture. Later on I have to go round the camp and collect the money for the fruit so the Chinese can be paid next time he comes.

This fellow also brings gula, a few eggs at thirty-three cents each, dry opak biscuits and, on odd occasions, baby onions, hard red beans, and bean flour, all of which we buy at a terrific price. Hence our labouring for a living to be able to buy these things.

Iole and I are now a kongsi of two—much, much easier, and less labour over those awful fires that smoke and never seem to have a flame. We started earning our living by making what we had the nerve to call banana fritters, which we sold in vast numbers to the N.E.I. inhabitants on the Dutch side of the camp. They were made mostly from gaplek flour, which we pounded, plus about three squashy bananas beaten to a pulp. They were quite good and very popular at ten cents each. Of course we had to buy the gaplek from those people who wouldn't eat the stuff and buy oil to cook them in. Then oil was stopped, so we scrapped that idea and made loaves of bread. Really, our nerve was colossal. We pounded soya beans and dried gaplek until we arrived at a mixture which, when water and salt were added, was pressed into bully-beef tins (which we also bought, empty, from those who had them) and steamed for half an hour.

All went well for a few weeks, then the gaplek was stopped. We were making enough money to buy all fruit rationed to us and an egg now and then, plus gula and red beans, and this helped considerably.

Stopping the gaplek set us thinking again, since we couldn't make any more "bread". We needed all the fruit and sugar we could get to work up enough energy to do this work, in addition to camp chores and wood-chopping.

My hair-cutting at ten cents a time was definitely not paying, so I had to put up my price to twenty cents if my customers had any money—if they didn't it was cut for nothing. Then Iole had the bright idea of making soup and selling it at night when people were hungry and cold and miserable. We had a garden of spinach, a few chillies, and beans, so this went into the soup. It flourished. It was ordered days before it was made, quite a lot of it going to convalescing hospital patients.

Then we ran out of beans and salt. At the moment we are bereft of a means of support, damned hungry, and can't afford to buy the things coming in the shop.

None of us are very happy today; it is exactly two years since our ship was bombed and we had to swim for it, losing so many of our friends of Malaya and Singapore days.

88

The Japs have left us for the time being, and we are again being guarded by Javanese Policie fellows, dozens of them, but this lot doesn't seem particularly fond of us. They say we are getting too much to eat! Our daily ration is eaten in five minutes, we are full for ten minutes, then spend the rest of the day just being hungry.

The Sumatras and storms have done quite a lot of damage. There are large pieces of attap roof missing on all the huts; even the hospital leaks. A week or so ago we were all amazed to see two nuns, Sister Catherinia and Sister Paulie, up on the roof, barefooted, long skirts hitched up and their large veils blowing in the wind almost at right angles, and patching the huge gaps with old rush mats. Nobody knows why they haven't fallen through a roof yet; they have been going up each day since our last storm, and appear to be quite happy about it.

We don't know where we would all be if we didn't have Sister Catherinia with us. She can do anything and is one of the outstanding personalities of the camp. She is a first-class electrician and would have given her boots to be in the navy, she told me. Instead, she entered a convent. She can speak in any language and works like a nigger. She is a wizard at fixing lights for concerts, and if the camp blacks out in a storm this sister soon has the lights going again.

We had only been in the "Men's Camp", as we call this place, a week or so when the four British sisters were returned to camp after being away for more than a year nursing in Palembang.

They looked terrible, and had a definitely wild look in in their eyes, which is not to be wondered at. They had been treated very badly by the Japanese and because of some infinitesimal wrong they had done they were put in jail. The Dutch wife of a doctor who had been working with these girls was also put in jail, each one in solitary confinement. There they sat on a cold floor with nothing to do all day but just sit, nothing to read or write, for six months. During the last few weeks they had two cells between five of them.

Amazingly enough, they were quite sane when they joined us again, but one lass had to go into our camp hospital for some weeks.

We were very relieved to have them back, for we had heard these girls were in the jail some months before, and we all wondered when, if ever, we would see them again. What a strong, healthy girl Margot Turner must be! She is a nursing sister in Queen Alexandra's Imperial Military Nursing Service, and had already had a shocking time getting from Singapore to Banka Island in February 1942. She was on a raft for five or six days before being picked up by a Japanese destroyer and brought to us at Muntok. Margot was a very sick girl for a long time.

An Irish girl, Sister Mary Cooper, also in jail for six months, was a member of Q.A.I.M.N.S.

March 1944. Have just celebrated Iole's third birthday in camp. She was given four "parties"—what we call parties, anyway. They are just ordinary rations glorified to look like what they aren't, plus a rice birthday cake about the size of an orange. (Oh, for an orange!) After tea we had our fourth party in the Dutch kitchen, girls from England, Ireland, Australia, New Zealand, and Holland were there. We had a wonderful "nassi goreng" (fried rice) and coffee, and for once all went to bed with full tummies.

What a difference it makes! We all slept well, instead of rolling round in empty agony. It is queer, but we go to bed hungry every night and the thought of food at home refuses to leave our minds. It is a great help to talk about what we should be having for dinner at home that night, or discussing recipes and how certain things are cooked. We often arrange a whole week of menus, saying we have each other as guests at our homes for a few days. It is really true that we find it hard to keep up with the saliva. "Makes our mouths water" is a fact! It positively runs, then after a few hours of this we have to get out and have a drink of water to fill our tummies before finally getting to sleep. In the morning we don't seem to be so desperately hungry, though it is fifteen hours since our last bowl of rice.

26th March 1944. Since the day of the four parties things have again changed. The Chinese bringing the fruit is now selling us the world's worst bananas, with thick velvety skins and a minute centre no bigger than my little finger. These are three cents each and can only be curried, skin and all. Gula comes once a month, and then at an impossible price, and the red beans are almost eaten away by weevils before we get them.

The wood for the fires is getting harder to cope with daily. We now get huge wet tree-trunks that have been felled only that day and are running with rubber latex and smothered with green leaves. We still have only the one blunt axe. We now have an axe roster.

Our dormitory has been divided into two parts, exactly in half, and boarded across. Twenty-six of us live in one half, and eight young Indonesians, who are training to be guards or Jap soldiers, or something, live in the other half. This isn't so good. We have all had to move up and our bed-space is now marked on the wooden ledge. You do *not* go over your line! Twenty and a half inches by five feet six inches and no air—it is terrific! It really is impossible in this hot, sticky climate, so some of the sisters are sleeping outside on the crude dinner benches, being slightly protected by the sloping roof of the hut. Four braves sleep in the children's shelter shed; they move around all night dodging the rain from the leaking attap roof. Believe me, we'll all be able to settle down very comfortably in any of those tram shelters along St Kilda Road when we get home.

The latest gossip is that Japanese military is going to look after us from now on, that they will take over on their famous date, 1st April. Something happens every year on that date. They promise us (*i*) extra bed-space, (*ii*) more food, and (*iii*) plenty more work. More work especially—we have been told by our lords and masters that we are women and should do more work, because after the war we shall have to work hard for the men, who will be so tired. Hell's bells, we can't work harder than we do now! We light, eventually, a fire to cook our rations, with wet, sappy wood, all smoke and no flame or heat. We honestly sit from 7 a.m. till 12 noon blowing our lungs out, and then all we have cooked is about a cupful of food. No wonder we all have slim figures, rice diet and sleeping on tiles for two years is the most effective slimming process I know. When we get home none of us ever intends to be hungry again; we now see eye to eye with Scarlett O'Hara!

A few days ago one of our English friends died. She had the most amazing knowledge and could talk on any subject. She loved reading, so set out to learn Dutch so she could read books in the camp Dutch library, which was much bigger than ours. She took only six weeks to learn the language.

The Jap guards wouldn't help us when she died, and would not bring in a coffin for more than twenty-four hours afterwards. It was a terrible thing to do in this overcrowded camp, so near to the Equator. Our friend was placed on a home-made stretcher and carried into the shelter shed in the middle of the camp, since we were not allowed to go outside. We watched in twos all through that night and next day, until somebody could locate a reasonable Jap who would help us.

They are not human, they are just beasts.

Chapter 16

7th April 1944. Well, Jap military took us over on April Fool's day all right, and what a show was turned on! Something new has happened every day so far.

First of all we had to gather in nationality groups and be presented to His Oriental Highness, Captain Siki. He is an awful-looking individual with a hard, staring brown eye, the other one being too bloodshot to see properly. We were also presented to his offsider, "Fattie", soon called "Ah Fat", who resembled a fat pig. There was a third Jap, who looked rather promising; his expression was different and he was quite a human type. We were announced one by one, and had to walk through the playground where these oddments were assembled, and bow. It was rather a scream really, because there was a very sticky patch of clay just where we had to bow, and so many of us came to grief and slipped or fell over their table when we hit this spot. The Japs were not amused, but we were. Poor old Tojo, nothing ever comes off with dignity and something always goes wrong. It's just women. Even the babies in the camp had to be presented, quite often long before their mothers. Although we stood all day none of us would have missed that show for anything.

After the introductions were over, in came sacks of decent rice, quite the best quality we have had so far. This, when divided, gave us a slightly larger ration—about three-quarters of a cup a day instead of half a cup. Sugar and salt also came. This sounds good, but the ration is a small teaspoon of sugar each daily and a little more salt. Still, we can't complain, it is good to see it coming in. Next day the vegetable ration dropped by half. Then in came ten sacks of filthy, weevily maize, which has now been thoroughly washed and dried and is very filling. It is good. We have also been given decent tea at last, a half cup per person per month. Also some queer curry powder. The maize helps a lot to ease off the old hunger pains and if pounded makes good porridge.

Next thing to arrive was a kerosene tin of red palm-oil for five hundred people. It is wonderful to be able to have something fried after months of no fat of any description. We sound as if we are living on the fat of the land, but these things are only enough to last a few days and we have to eke them out to last for a month. We haven't sighted soap for months and are a fine colour! When it rains we still dash out and stand under the nearest piece of leaking roof, the only decent wash we can get.

Two days ago, when we were having a rest after lunch, we heard a heavy truck coming up the road outside. All heads bobbed up and all eyes were glued to our own special cracks and peep-holes in the wooden walls. Someone called, "Wood!" and we all relaxed again. Suddenly an excited call went up, "European women!" The air was electric—could there be some more of our girls. We all got up at once and hurried over to the main entrance. During our stay here Indo-Dutch and Indonesians have been brought in at odd times, but these were the first Britishers we have seen since we were interned.

We knew only one, she had been Matron of the British General Hospital in Malacca where we had our hospital, too, in 1941.

A few of the new-comers were British sisters; there were also a Scottish doctor, three Dutchwomen, and a few Eurasians. We now have four women doctors in camp here.

These people had come from a small camp at Djambi, a place farther north in Sumatra. Of course, the first thing was interchange of news. We told them some they hadn't heard, and they did the same for us. Naturally, we all had to move up and make more room. If only the "hee-haws" or the "hay-hoes" or whatever it is these Indonesian trainees are called would get out of our block!

They are not having a very happy time. A few days ago a Jap N.C.O. came in and beat one fellow very badly, smacking his face with a knotted handkerchief wrapped round his fist. Then he forced the "hee-haw" back against the wall by holding and pressing an enamel plate into his mouth. Ugh, it was horrible to watch!

22nd April 1944. More excitement. Sister James was asked to go to the guard-house. She came back in a minute to say we all had to go, so thirty-two of us set off with very queer sensations going through us. What did they want this time?

We had to write our names and army numbers on a pad, and those who had them produced identification discs. An old Jap—a colonel, we thought—spoke to us in English. He was very like Charlie Chaplin and was immediately called that. He proceeded to tell us a story about Jap submarines entering Sydney Harbour and doing great damage to the *Queen Mary* and *Queen Elizabeth*, also damaging the centre pylon of the Harbour Bridge. We relaxed slightly; it hasn't got a centre pylon!

However, we were just too popular because the Japs in the submarines lost their lives and their ashes had been sent back to Tokyo. Wilma Oram wished under her breath that they would send our bones back to Australia, with us outside them.

After a while he smiled at us.

"Something very good is coming to you," he said.

We all smiled and nodded our approval.

"It couldn't be worse, could it?"

"No," we all replied quite heartily.

"All right, you wait and be good." And off the little fellow went. It is little comfort to know they are ashamed of themselves and of what they haven't done for us. Well, here's hoping "something good" is this mercy ship we hear so much about, and which never arrives. We all want to get out of this so badly.

28th April 1944. It is rats and spiders now. Rats are as big as kittens and race over us all night long. "Midnight", the black cat without a tail who has attached himself to the camp, is doing his best, but insists on leaving rat carcasses on our shelves, usually resting on our few belongings and clothing oddments.

Iole was wakened last night by a swishing noise under her ear, so she shook her small pillow and a huge spider ran up her mosquito net. Its body was as large as the palm of her hand. We found it next morning over on Mavis Hannah's bed-space, just opposite, but the thing disappeared while somebody was getting a piece of wood to kill it.

30th April 1944. Today I was so hungry that I could hardly walk. The first time it has hit me like this. Iole and I literally hadn't a thing we could eat. All our tins were empty—rice, sugar, corn, all gone. Iole spent the morning lying on her bed-space, and I just flopped on my part of the table outside and prayed for death or something to eat. At midday my prayers were answered, and along came rations of rice, corn, sugar, salt, curry powder, and oil. All in tiny quantities, but it is food. We felt better very quickly after cooking a little rice. We are both trying to recuperate after an attack of dengue fever.

Since the military people have taken us over we have been weighed twice. It doesn't help really to know that we are losing weight. Not one of us weighs much over seven stone.

There have been three further inquiries about us thirty-two

since the day Charlie Chaplin came, so we kid ourselves that our ship is on the horizon.

Iole and I have had another attack of something. Both developed a temperature and aches and pains very suddenly. Then I produced the most glorious-looking rash. Somebody sent for Dr McDowell, but by the time she arrived the rash had cooled down and disappeared. Thank God the other girls saw it, or I would be fearing for my sanity! It is awful being sick under these conditions and is so uncomfortable lying all day and night on hard wooden boards with nothing underneath for protection. We two have decided to "employ" somebody to cook our rice for us for a week while we get over this. That means someone is working for us instead of us working for them.

8th May 1944. We were visited by two Japanese nurses who walked round the camp today, holding hankies to their flat noses. They looked awful in their uniforms. They wore long white dresses, almost to their ankles, and peculiar hats. I was doing bathroom-squad chores, pulling water up from a well, dragging it into the bathroom, and tossing it on the floor, while our Del and an English sister scraped away with a bundle of old sticks bound together to try to clean the place a bit. When the two nurses came near me I stood aside and did my piece nobly for these daughters of Nippon, and bowed till I cracked and said, "Morning", but no, they would have none of me. They merely held their handkerchiefs a little more firmly to their noses, took a wide circle away from me, and walked on towards the kitchens. I wonder what we really look like? Do we smell?

They must have been impressed with the mixture of nationalities we have here amongst these women. And all would rather be here behind barbed wire than be with the Japanese. There are English, Scottish, Irish, American, Canadian, New Zealand, South African, Dutch, French, German, Russian, Austrian, Swiss, Latvian, Icelandic, Indian, Singalese, Chinese, Siamese, Malay, Javanese, Balinese, Indonesian, Indo-Dutch, and Eurasian women—and us. And we all have the same enemy! Three languages are spoken, English, Malay, and Dutch, and always Malay when speaking with the Japanese. At one stage the Nips insisted on our learning "Nippon-Go", but we wouldn't play. We asked for paper and pencils, which they refused, so we refused to learn it.

Ah Fat visits us a lot. He lives next door now in the guardhouse, so spends quite a lot of time watching the industry going on here, most of it trying to keep body and soul together. He insists on calling our new British commandant, Mrs Hinch, "Inchi", and comes screaming through Block 7, where Mrs Hinch lives, "Inchi! Inchi!" Mrs Hinch emerges, serene and calm, and with a most dignified, bored expression on her face asks him what he wants. Everyone who hears this, of course, can hardly keep a straight face until he has gone.

20th May 1944. What a lot has happened since I last wrote! We have been forced to go outside the camp and tidy up overgrown gardens round the neighbourhood. We asked for axes, but they sent in chungkals, weighing about twenty-two pounds each; we could hardly lift them. They are like large hoes with heavy iron heads and thick wooden handles. Seventy-two of these things arrived, but still no axes. Our old original blunt one still cuts wood for us all. Out we go in squads and chungkal away at this jungle, and is the ground hard? We can hardly make an impression. It is feet high with weeds and oddments and snakes are laid on.

People took to this rather well, since it is one way of letting our feelings go a bit, and the novelty of having something to do that is different from camp chores is a great help. The place was flourishing with gardens, inside and out, in no time.

"Seedling", the Jap officer with the "different" face, has brought many seeds and young cuttings, hence his name. He is a reasonable little fellow, speaks a little English, and is always pleasant.

Iole and I have made two gardens in our corner of the camp. They are about six feet long and three feet wide and looked a bit like graves at first, but not now that things are growing there. We grow spinach, corn, tomatoes, tapioca, and long beans. There is a border of balsam flowers, so the corner looks quite gay. We are growing a small lawn round it at the moment, which we trim with a knife blade. We have built a tiny table so we can eat our breakfast and evening meal away from the madding crowd. We bought a serviette from a Dutch woman, which we use as a table-cloth, and have half a coconut shell full of balsam flowers on the table, our food bowls and a spoon each. We feel quite civilized.

It has made a big difference to have our own little garden of vegetables and balsam flowers growing so fast. Fortunately we kept some tomato and balsam seeds from our small garden in the last camp in case we were moved suddenly to another camp and would want to start a garden. The tomatoes are delicate-looking plants but are growing fairly well. Other seeds we scrounged from the kitchen from rotting vegetables that had been discarded by the cooks. The spinach was a try-out, really. It is real spinach and came only once in the rations, so we collected the roots after the cooks had taken the rest and put them in the ground. To our amazement they are growing well.

Every day now somebody comes or something exciting occurs. Who said internment was boring? We get a great kick out of their camp inspections by officers. They are so serious and they look so unlike officers as we know them. They wear little caps on top of their shaven heads, short badly fitting coats with their rank often pinned on with a safety pin, shorts, suspenders, socks, and slippers, plus a large dangling sword! Their pants are patched more often than not.

A little while ago, to our amazement, we were all *paid*!! What a thrill to have some money! We were given four guilders fifty cents each. They promise to pay us this amount each month, which works out at about two shillings a week. After the money, food arrived for us to buy. There were little sweet biscuits that melted away to nothing as soon as they hit our mouths, nine cents each; boiled sweets at one cent each.

One Sunday a car drove up and a Jap deposited on the

ground a large soempit which moved and flopped around! On opening it we found fresh fish. They were beautiful fish; any angler would have been proud of them. The Dutch children were wildly excited; some of them had never seen a live fish and they raced all over the camp calling, "*Vis, vis!*" That ration worked out at three-quarters of a fish each, the first protein we have had for twelve months.

A few days later in came thirty live fowls, definitely internees, too, by the look of their figures, and how we got to work on them! We had a squad to kill, pluck and clean them, then cut them and put them into one large stew. All their insides were cooked separately, so we had poultry twice in one day. It worked out at one fowl to eighteen people, but we all had a few mouthfuls of actual meat, and later a cupful of chicken broth. Things are looking up. All the same, we find we can easily fit into our 20½-inch bed-space now.

Duck-eggs are coming in at the rate of one each a week, often bad, for which we pay thirty-eight cents, but they are good to have. Even a bad duck-egg makes a good omelet!

So ends the four guilders fifty cents. It is only lent to us.

Norah's "orchestra" practises in the Dutch kitchen two nights a week now. Norah must beg permission to sing from the guard on duty. He wants to know why we can sing while our people are being killed.

Have just had my third birthday in captivity and it was a day full of surprises. Flowers arrived arranged in coconut shells (with a note to please return the shell), a camp-made mah-jongg set with the Chinese characters painted by Kong, the flowers, each one common to the camp, painted by Dutch Rita, the rest done by New Zealander Audrey Owen. It was all packed neatly away in a handsome little box made from a soempit, and was quite perfect. Audrey came along and presented it and made an awfully long speech. We thought if she didn't stop we would have to ask her to breakfast. Norah gave me a drawing of the Australian kitchen, which stands better on paper than it does in real life. Iole gave me a real breakfast. She set our table in the garden, producing two cups and two saucers and a teapot. Heaven knows where these came from. We had our usual rice porridge and I thought it was all over, but then came the big surprise. Fried rice bread, fried egg, and the first spinach from our garden. It was a sumptuous meal and we were the envy of all.

It was the first time we have been able to connect with everything. Usually it is egg but no oil to fry it, or oil and no egg, but it went well this day for once. We had a dinner party that night and invited Dot Freeman and Rene Singleton who are the opposition in the bakery business we carry on. We four call ourselves "Australian Bakeries Limited", but work in twos, comparing and sampling and helping each other to fulfil orders round the camp.

This was the menu. We were lucky that fish came that day.

1. Cocktail made from fermented rice, gula, and limejuice—excellent.
2. Fried rice-bread sandwiches with fish paste. (The paste was made from fish bones and heads, roasted, pounded, and mixed with salt, pepper, oil and limejuice.)
3. Steamed fish and camp-model white sauce.
4. Fried rice as near to nassi goreng as possible.
5. Coffee pudding, steamed in a small bully-beef tin.
6. Black coffee with *sugar*.

What a dinner! It was worth all the saving that had gone on the week before.

H

Chapter 17

24th May 1944. A couple of days ago "Ah Fat" suddenly arrived on the scene in his yellow pyjamas and slippers, and asked for six strong women from each dormitory. Nobody knew what he wanted them for, but some braves took off trustingly and came back a few minutes later carrying huge iron vat things they call "kwalis". This means community cooking for the British. The Dutch have been having community cooking ever since they came to this camp, while the British had small fires going every few yards up and down the British "lines", with a resulting mess and complete untidiness everywhere. We couldn't do anything else, since we didn't have anything large enough for community cooking. "Ah Fat" told us to strip the poor rickety old Australian kitchen, and to build four fireplaces. There was nothing to build them with, so we had to strip dozens of the smaller fires and take what bricks and stones would fit together. They were stuck together with clay, of which there was plenty near the well-head.

Two huge fireplaces were built in no time, then somebody had a better idea, and by 5 p.m. we had pulled down many walls and opened up a large space alongside the Dutch kitchen, so we could have both kitchens under the one roof. As the camp is old and made of attap it wasn't hard to do. Three fireplaces were built of broken bricks, stones, mud, and clay, and, as we were not allowed to light small fires again, Mrs Tops, known to us all as Sally, who is O.C. Dutch kitchen, suggested they should cook for the whole camp for twenty-four hours and so allow our fireplaces to dry. Good for you, Sally!

We then had to call block meetings to work our squads—rice cooks, vegetable cooks, wood-choppers, water-carriers, servers, washers-up, vegetable cutters, bathroom squad, ration officers, etc. Quite a business, now everybody had a set job and all pulled their weight.

Yesterday we were all called into the central playground because Captain Siki wished to say a few words. Charlie Chaplin was with him again. Siki usually stands on a table and, with a fierce look in his eye, speaks to us in straight Japanese, which is not very enlightening. It is then interpreted into Malay, and Mrs Hinch passes it on to all the British. We could tell the boys were in a good mood yesterday and seemed to be friendly towards us. They said we were to be more tidy in the dormitories, to put our cabin trunks together in one place and not have too many dresses hanging up and so on. They would inspect us two days later.

We dashed inside, folded our uniforms neatly, and were ready for inspection!

Later Siki spoke again. He told us to expect a few bombs, but that they would look after us. They would arrange to take us into the rubber for safety in an emergency. They also told us some fool idea of how to keep mosquitoes away while out in the rubber.

This is certainly the first time Siki has shown us any consideration; however, we shall see if he means it. Siki said he would die with us in the rubber, so we all cheered him! He was nonplussed.

11th July 1944. Had to hide my diary again, for six weeks this time.

Three more British women have died. If only the Nips would give us quinine and something to stop dysentery.

More changes. Pay has stopped already, and now we have what Nippon has the nerve to call a bank account! Instead of getting our money for the month we had three bananas, a small piece of green pineapple, and a cup of sugar. No biscuits, no boiled sweets, less food all round, but fresh fish still on Sundays—for the last few Sundays, anyway. Everything else has been cut and at this stage we are craving for something sweet. A while ago all we wanted was "one of mum's steak-and-kidney pies"; at the moment all we ask for are honey, treacle, golden syrup, plus lots of sugar and a cream cake. All the Victorians here have promised to shout the Sydney and Brisbane girls afternoon tea at "The Wattle" in Melbourne, famous for its luscious cream cakes.

For the last two months we have lived on three bowls of rice each day, with kang kong leaves as a vegetable at midday and their stalks, cut like French beans, for the evening meal. These stalks have bitter white sap, like thistles, in them. They are hard to get down, but we manage it. For a while we had curry made of banana skins, which was purple when cooked, but now we have green pineapple instead of banana and it is better. We make cordial with pineapple skins and excellent scrubbing brushes with their scraggy tops.

The latest Jap idea for vegetables is to eat jungle. A fellow took some of our people out and showed them which was edible and which was poisonous, so we now eat wild vines, the leaves of dahlias, and most grasses.

There is nothing worse than being constantly hungry. Eggs go to hospital patients only; at the moment they get three a day. We get mad every now and then to think of some people who have never done a hand's turn in camp getting three eggs a day in hospital, while we do all the work and don't get eggs because we are "well".

Siki the Sadist came into camp and delivered some more Jap chat to us a week or so ago. He says he can't get any more food for us and we must grow our own. After September rice will be almost non-existent. Siki says we must take life more seriously, sing less, and dig more gardens. Gardening squads are now formed, the same old hard-working few, and the same old "passengers" with what they call their "hearts", who can't work. Guess nobody has a normal heart at this stage! The "hearts" get any odd eggs from hospital for staying at home, while the workers dig for victory on an empty stomach, wielding these twenty-two-pound chungkals for at least one hour every day.

Now the whole of the inside of the camp, and outside, too, has been "chungkalled" into gardens of sweet potatoes and tapioca. Even the roadside and gardens and lawns in private houses in the district around us have turned into potato patches by our efforts.

It is amazing how good we are at "government stroke", and unless the guards are watching carefully we can quickly jump back into the row behind, which has been done, and look as if we are working hard. Nasty little Ito watches like a hawk and examines our hands for blisters. If we have blisters, we are working and are "bagus" ("good"); if we haven't any blisters Ito stays alongside to see we do raise some.

Planting sweet potatoes is an eye-opener. We had all the ground ready in small furrows, and at 5 p.m. one night Seedling and Ito came in with bundles of green sweet-potato cuttings and we had to plant them at once and water them. Some cuttings had flowers on them. The boys promise us potatoes in three months! Maybe! Tapioca is planted by cutting eight-inch lengths from the stalk of a fully grown plant, and pushing these into the ground at an angle. Leaves appear in two days!

Even now Ito is desperate for places for us to work in, so we have to weed the roads and street drains, which are deep, overgrown, and filthy. Nobody has any energy at all these days, except that bit kept to do our own chores, which are many and getting more difficult.

Iole and Wilma have developed into the best rice cooks in the camp, while Sylvia Muir, Tweedie, and I are washing up for them from 5.30 a.m. until 6 p.m. one day in three. We are all on the same cooking squad so we can get to our jobs and earn our living on the other two days.

The only French internee with us is Mrs Gilmour. She is in charge of one of the three British cooking squads and produces the most intriguing sambals from cucumber, curry stuffs, and oddments. Mrs Gilmour is a very quiet, sweet soul; we all like her very much. She was interned during the last war when she was a child and now the Japanese have caught up with her in this war. What interesting things she has told us from time to time! We have a fellow feeling, she is married to a Digger. Some of us have brushed up our school French with her; she nearly has fits at our efforts, but it does help to keep our minds ticking over all the time. It would be so easy to flop round the place and relax completely, but as well as being hopelessly boring this would not do anybody any good.

Our latest trouble is lack of water. We should be used to it by this time, after hunting in people's back yards for two years in search of a bucket of water, but here we are locked in and the three wells can't supply us. Two wells belong to the Dutch and one to the British. As there are many more Dutch here than British, that is, of course, always the division in everything. The wells are almost dry now and only a little water seeps through at night. The ration is a five-pound butter tin per person per day, and we have to line up in a queue, each block at a time, for our ration. If only it would rain! We have not had any for weeks; rain clouds come, but blow over again. Everything is as hot as the devil and dry as chips. Next war we have all decided to set off at once for the South Pole with plenty of clothes and some sugar!

Nothing further has been done about us. All their wonderful promises—"it can't be worse". Poor, pathetic us, we almost believed them! It has been ten times worse since that statement, "Something very good will come for you." It did, those heavy chungkals to do coolie labour. Their ambition is to make us white coolies.

The latest idea is for us to unload and carry sacks of rice into the camp when the ration comes, while natives sit round smoking straws and watch and laugh at us. One day last week we had to unload a truck full of rice and store it in a Jap garage near by. There were at least fifty heavy sacks. They do loathe us and get so mad when we chat brightly and organize a system to make the job easier.

A Scottish woman was called out to the centre of the camp today by a guard. She doesn't know what she did to annoy him, but she stood there facing up to him as he prepared to whack her hard across the face. Suddenly she called to him to stop; he did so, and she whipped off her glasses and removed a denture, then stood facing him again. He was puzzled for a moment, then threw back his head and laughed and walked away. It was priceless to watch.

A fowl, Palembang model, flew over the fence from the Jap guard-house alongside our kitchen. There was a mad rush by a few Australian and English sisters. Margot Turner was first to get it. In two minutes the unfortunate bird was in our block and we were discussing if we should kill it or put it back over the fence. After all, it did belong to the guards. We also discussed whether we could cook it without the smell going round the camp. Margot was holding it by the legs and keeping its beak shut to stop its noise, when suddenly the fowl closed its eyes and went limp in her hands. Margot's face was a study; she was sure she had killed it, so let it go. The wily old bird flew under the bed-space platform and it took us ages to get it out. There was no delay then; it was killed, de-feathered, and into the pot in a few minutes. That night the English and Australian sisters had chicken soup and stew for dinner.

Banana-skin curries are taboo. One of the Japs' "girl-friends" told the Jap rations officer what we were giving her in the community cooking, so all bananas were stopped. However, we continue to go without the main essentials in an ordinary diet; we must be made of cast iron. All the same, there are always about thirty people in the camp hospital, and about fifty ill in the blocks. We live from day to day, nobody bothers about what will happen next week. Why worry? We can't do anything about it.

26th July 1944. "Rasputin" has arrived and joined "The Snake" to annoy us a little more. He is definitely turning on the agony. We haven't had any rain for over a month, and all wells are dry. The tap is allowed to trickle for a couple of hours each day and nearly six hundred women and children have to be bathed, fed, watered, and clothes washed, but more important, says Rasputin, are those sweet potatoes we planted in the middle of the camp a while ago. They must be watered.

At the hottest hour of the day, 1 p.m., when even the natives sleep, we have to stand in the sun for half an hour and wait for tenko, then, when it pleases the guard, we move off and out of camp to the road, carrying anything that will hold water, buckets on poles if we have them. We walk a long way before we come to the back gate of the camp. From there we turn into a street full of Jap houses, eventually getting into the main road, where we lived for two months early in 1942. Down a hill on a very stony road we trudge, barefooted, until we come to a pump surrounded with mud and filth. A queue is organized and two of our people "jaga" the pump to keep law and order.

Back we come up hill with the water and are forced to throw it on the sweet potatoes. It must be a good half-mile easily, and I hate to think how many trips we make. If only we had protection for our feet! We can manage at odd times to get a little dirty water from one well; we asked Rasputin and Ito if we could change it for the clean water we were carrying, and so put well water on the potatoes and have the clean water for ourselves. Absolutely no!

Yesterday we were told that a very important and high Japanese official is coming and we must clean up the camp. Even the black smuts on the kitchen attap roof must be cleaned. Old sheds have to come down, and all must be in order. We had to do drains out in the streets and cut the long grass on the roadside and in the Jap gardens. "Looney the Dill" produced a lawn-mower and instructed a couple of our girls on how to use it. Their effort was most amusing, starting with a frightened look at the little mower and muttering, "*Apa?*" ("What is that?") Looney, in Malay, apparently told them not to be worried and showed them how to use it. He ran it up and down a strip of lawn. The girls knew how to block the mower, and did so, then sat down in the shade and waited for him to come back. He came soon, and they told him it was sick. He unstuck it and did two more strips to show them how easy it was, then handed the thing over to them. He went away and once more they jammed it and went off and sat down. Again poor Looney came to their aid. He still hasn't realized he cut the whole lawn!

Five of us had to clean out a Jap storehouse, managed to spill some rice, and were allowed to bring it home. Today we have to empty the contents of the septic tank on those so-and-so sweet potatoes. We hope fervently we are not asked to eat them later on.

28th July 1944. A young English girl, a member of the camp choral society, died very suddenly yesterday. She was apparently quite well and was working the kitchen with her squad a few days ago. Then suddenly she collapsed and was taken to the hospital, where she died. This has rocked the whole camp, for she was only in her twenties and considered one of the healthiest people here. She was a darling and will be missed very much by us all.

The "high official" duly arrived this morning, and we have never seen our Rasputin and guards in such a complete dither. He is certainly the most important one we have had so far. We wonder who he is. He was very fat, and very badly dressed in a little, short, badly made coat, patched pants, red and gold everywhere, and carried a huge sword. We were not allowed to speak to him; nobody had any desire to do so. He moved slowly round the camp and we all did our stuff by bowing, then he left after spending fully five minutes with us. "How much for sixpence?" we all asked each other. We should have liked a loan of his car for an hour or so; it was a beautiful looking thing.

After lunch Siki the Sadist wasted one and a half hours making yet another speech in Japanese. We still haven't a clue as to what he was saying. Two people apparently did understand, and when I asked one of them what it was all about she said, "Och, it was nothing." What a waste of time!

8th August 1944. We had ten minutes of glorious rain today, the first for nearly six weeks, so most of us had a bath under the leaking roofs and washed our hair. Let's hope the wells fill a little now, this butter tin of water a day is a bit hard to manage with. We all feel we are beginning to smell a little like the drains round the place, which Jennie Greer insists on calling "4711".

Rasputin is turning things on. He is a devil. We now go water-carrying for those flaming sweet potatoes every day. After the gardens are finished we have to fill the water tanks in the community kitchen, then we may bring one for ourselves. How tiring it all is in this hot sun! We now have dysentery and another typhoid patient in the little camp hospital. Not so good.

We, who get filthy living in this awful place, and have to ration ourselves so strictly with water, now have to carry the stuff up to the Jap houses in the next street for them to bathe their nasty little bodies. They throw at least four bucketfuls which we have to carry, over themselves, and we also have to keep their tongs full. We often wonder if we shall ever be rescued from this or if we are completely forgotten.

You can't go far in this camp without seeing something to laugh at. Great excitement behind the Dutch kitchen today. Somebody took a peep through a crack in the fence into a

Jap back yard, and there was Ah Fat, wrapped in a sarong, standing in a tub of water far too small for himself, having a nice warm bath in the sunshine. The tub was standing on bricks and had a little fire underneath to keep it warm. We were nearly splitting our sides. Poor old Fattie! He always looks so miserable. He told us he hates war and wants to go home to Japan to his wife and five children. We want to go home, too.

Yesterday four water-carriers were bringing in buckets of water as usual, when the Snake suddenly stopped them and made them stand in the sun on the veranda of the guard-house outside the camp, while he baited them in broken English.

"Say you are sorry."

One of them replied, "For what?"

"Say you are sorry," he said again.

"For what?" came the reply once more.

The Snake was furious and gave one of the women such a crashing blow across her face that she fell over the veranda wall, which is about four feet high, and on to the lawn. Her face was still red hours later.

Each hour he reappeared to ask the women if they were sorry, and each time they replied that they were not sorry, because they had not done anything wrong. He kept sneering at them, "You British!"

When darkness fell, and after the British and Dutch commandants had been in to see the Snake, these poor weary people were sent back into camp with instructions to get up at 6 a.m. and "fertilize" these dreadful potatoes and the gardens surrounding the outside of the camp, until the Snake came in to see them. This is the latest punishment for simply "being British". By "fertilizing", they mean that we must go outside armed with a leaking kerosene tin and a half-tin nailed to a stick, proceed to the septic tank, fill the kerosene tin with its contents, bring it back *into* camp and put it on the gardens. What sweet little minds these Japs have! We have to do this every day; it dries, and the wind blows the dust all over us and into everything. No wonder we have typhoid and dysentery in the camp.

These four people were up and on the job at 6 a.m. this morning, and after three hours the Snake came in and told them they could stop. He said that they had been punished, and presented each one with a cake of soap and some Chinese biscuits. We'll win this war yet!

10th August 1944. Found myself on the 6 a.m. squad to go "gardening" this morning. There were eight Dutch people and four British. The British consisted of an Englishwoman, a Chinese, a dark-skinned child from Malaya, and myself. We lined up for tenko at the guard-house, dressed in shorts and sun-top only as usual, complete with heavy chungkals and empty stomachs. We awaited the pleasure of Ito, a conceited, ugly little man with a huge jaw. Ito was very pleased with himself and asked the British to stand apart, then motioned the Dutch to move outside and down the road with another guard. We four proudly stepped forward, and Ito removed our chungkals. At first we thought the Japs had beaten the British in a battle somewhere, and we were going to be let off. Not so, we were taken outside to the rubbish pit which smells so much and is so filthy it practically stands on end. We sank up to our knees in the squashy stuff and were told to remove it about four hundred yards along the road in the leaking kerosene tins used by the "sanitary squad" and dump it in the back garden of the house where the Jap guards sleep. This was too good to be true! We "misunderstood" them, and the English girl and I gathered the worst part of that foul mess, carried it down the road to that house, and dumped it on the lawn under the Snake's window. There were rotting pine-apple tops, old rags, broken china, soggy cigarette butts, hair, filthy rotting ends of rations, and squashy fluid. It was disgusting. We did this for about an hour, so when the sun reaches it it should be grand. We were nearly knocked sideways gathering it.

Ito decided we were not taking it seriously enough, so made us adjourn to the septic tank and fertilize the sweet potatoes on the side of the camp farthest from the tank. We carried filth barefooted for miles that morning. I feel I will never be clean again.

Our "protectors", as the Japanese call themselves, are the best bunch of cut-throats we have ever seen. They are surely hand-picked for this job. What an unattractive race, rather like monkeys! There has been a succession of guards: Banana Johnnie, George, Lipstick Larry, Rasputin, the Snake, Fattie or Ah Fat, Seedling, Almond Eyes, Bully, the Student (a sadist if ever there was one), Billy the Abortion and, of course, our hut neighbours, the hee-haws or hay-hoes. When tenko was to take place we hurried or dawdled into line according to which guard was on and how drunk he was at that moment. We are all getting quite shrewd, but would give anything in the world to see a sun-tanned Digger. Slit eyes and bandy legs are most uninteresting.

Chapter 18

11th August 1944. The most important date so far. It is terribly thrilling, something has happened at last.

Could not get to sleep last night, which is most unusual for me, and twisted and turned on my little bed-space for hours. I heard a clock in the guard-house strike one, and later half past one, then I thought I could hear planes in the distance—planes with a very different sound and more than I had ever heard before. I couldn't make it out. Japanese planes practised at night, but never after 9 p.m. The noise came nearer, so I woke Iole and told her to listen. Then we both heard that never to be forgotten "crr-u-u-mp" of falling bombs. Then the town sirens screamed and whined and the Japs went mad. It certainly caught them on the hop. Out went all lights in the camp area, then the real noise started. Ack-ack, whistles of shells, and all the fireworks and noise of Singapore once again. It was terrific.

We all jumped out from under our drooping mosquito nets and sat outside at the mess tables and watched the whole thing. They came in waves until it was almost daylight. Oh, the thrill of it, and what it means! There was one amusing incident, the dash for the one and only tin hat, which is used as the only floor-washing bucket in our block. As it was full of precious water nobody used it.

We sat the night out at those tables, all wildly excited and discussing it all. There was no point staying inside those flimsy attap huts with only one door at each end. Very few of our girls admitted it, but I know their knees were knocking with excitement, as mine were. Del was the only one to admit it.

This air raid rather fits in with the latest rumours—"Only one more week", and, "It must be over at the end of this month." We couldn't believe it, for everything seems as usual here, but now we do feel it won't be long. The scared stiff hay-hoes told us Pladjoe oilfield was heavily bombed.

This morning the Japs spread a rumour through the camp that last night's raid was practice. I have just been talking to Del, who is busy outside chopping away at some wood.

"So it was practice after all last night, Del?"

"Practice my foot!" said she. "My legs don't shake for practice."

15th August 1944. We had another raid two nights later, but nothing happened. We are all ready to grab our belongings and make a dash if it should be necessary. Our belongings make an excellent pillow. We are still waiting, but what a difference, knowing it is our own men bombing this time! We must look like an old swamp from up there where the planes are. We are not allowed to hang our washing on the lines outside now, which certainly clears the camp a lot, and we can walk upright to the kitchen or over to the Dutch lines instead of stooping the whole way to dodge people's washing on the lines.

We all hope our men shoot straight; it would be wretched luck to get a smack after all this.

It was rather amusing about the celebration of the first big raid. As it was Iole's sister's birthday, we had two things to celebrate, so we uprooted our famous tapioca plant. For weeks it has been growing very tall and was higher than the fence and really taking up too much room. We had eaten all its leaves as far as we could reach them, so we now ate its fleshy roots. They look rather like large dahlia roots with a thick skin and are very good to eat. This, added to our rations, was very filling.

Community cooking gives us rice porridge, a small bowl for breakfast at 7 a.m. Cooks call this mess "boeboer", we call it "boobo". It is one part rice and about six or eight parts water, in other words, a thick soup. Black coffee is served at 10 a.m. At midday a small bowl of rice with a dessertspoon of kang kong stalks and a teaspoon of sambal is given to us. This sambal is very popular; it is a highly flavoured type of seasoning made from anything in the rations with chilli or curry stuffs added. At 5 p.m. we have another bowl of rice with a teaspoon of kang kong leaves and a dessertspoon of cucumber stew. After that we sit around the camp in sociable groups and drink our black coffee made from the same grounds as the morning coffee, and, if anyone has that black native tobacco, smoke a cigarette.

Things might be awful inside this camp, but the sunsets at night are a joy for ever. We sit there and watch the most beautiful colour and cloud formations, changing every minute and each change more beautiful than the one before. Miss Dryburgh wrote a wonderful little poem called "Look Up", which was very inspiring.

No rain for ages, so water-carrying squads are properly organized to go on that midday crocodile march to the pump down in the main road. Even small children go, for every drop of water helps, and the queue contains buckets, tins, kettles, bottles, saucepans—anything that holds water. The last few days we have been rationed to a beer-bottle of water each, and no bath water, but we still have to carry enough to fill all the Jap bathrooms twice a day. The effort to do this is just about killing these people in this heat and in their half-starved condition.

The mothers of small children and babies are frantic without water to wash their children and their few clothes. We always seem to have babies in the camp. Nearly every fresh group that joins us here seems to bring a baby with them. It must be ghastly for the mothers.

When the Jap houses have been watered, and our community kitchen has enough, according to Ito, we then collect more for these awful gardens, which to our way of thinking is pure bloody-mindedness! However, we do manage to have a wash while carrying water up the road. We carry it sometimes on our shoulders and tip it over ourselves by accident, which helps a lot to cool us down.

Most of us are earning our own living now, and what a variety of talent there is amongst us! Win Davis and Pat Gunther make the most enchanting hats from the rush bags the fish comes in, using bits and pieces of material. They are really very snappy hats. Mavis Hannah has borrowed a sewing machine from a Dutch woman, and makes garments for young and old all day, when not doing her camp chores, from already worn-out clothes. Mavis makes a dashing pair of shorts, the 1944 slim figure sometimes looks quite smart! Win made seven pairs of black shorts from a nun's gown given to us some time ago, and gave a pair each to seven of us who were wearing through the patches on already patched shorts.

Quite a number of our girls go over to the Dutch lines and do their laundry and clean out their bed-space and do their chores, so earning enough to be in a position to say, "Yes, please", to an odd egg or banana or gula which may happen along. Iole was washer-woman and nursemaid to a Dutch family consisting of a mother and four small children for some months. It took two of us ages to get through that daily wash, and on the days when I couldn't help it took Iole from 6 a.m. till 8.30 a.m. just to get the washing out in the sun. Later she would take the children for a walk round the camp, not very interesting, then later on bring in the dry

clothes. All this for two and a half guilders a week! Fortunately, the Japanese and Chinese accept Straits dollars and
Dutch currency, though any change we might get is given
to us in Japanese paper money.

Val Smith was the only shoe-mender. She dragged home an
old piece of armchair found on the side of the road one day
when she was water-carrying. We all thought she was crazy,
but then she told us it was full of one-inch nails, which she
proceeded to pull out and put away in a small tin. Val made
a lot of money with those nails. She mended trompers, crude
slippers made of wood with a piece of rubber tubing or tyre
nailed across the toes to keep them on. These came apart or
broke all day long in the mud and sticky clay, so Val kept
herself in petty cash by adjusting broken straps at ten cents
a nail, two nails to each tromper, sometimes four.

Flo Trotter and I cut hair madly all day long, usually with
curved nail scissors, which kept us very busy.

Some sisters carried water for the Dutch at so much a
bucket. Del, being a champion at wood-chopping, wore out a
pair of shorts every few weeks chopping wood for dozens
of people. Nobody knows how that girl does it; she certainly
has it down to a fine art. A grand lass, Del.

Pounding gaplek and soya beans, making "milk" and
"cheese" from soya beans, brought in some income for some
sisters while others made bean cake called "tempi". It was
fermented soya beans growing a grey beard. Full of vitamins
and really very pleasant to eat when fried.

Sister Raymont, known to us all as Ray, is not at all well,
so she has to earn her living in a much more gentle fashion.
If she hurries about the place or water-carries she faints and
is then quite ill for some days getting over it. Consequently
we do not allow Ray to do anything at all, which rather
annoys her. So she sits and sews. She is able to keep herself in
petty cash by making the prettiest little handkerchiefs out of
bits and pieces, which are quickly snapped up by those people
here who have plenty of money.

Woodie makes the most fascinating rag dolls, which are

a credit to her and terribly popular with the children. She was forced to sell the R.A.A.F. greatcoat she found so early in our camp days because it was getting too heavy for her to cope with. She sold it to a Japanese officer and made him pay a huge sum for it. She is the most amusing girl; she didn't attempt to speak to him in Malay, but somehow he understood what she meant, because he came back with the money for her.

A good watch would bring anything from one hundred to one hundred and fifty Straits dollars, and anything gold was snapped up very smartly by the Japs. One sister was very hard up, and could not make up her mind whether to sell her four false teeth on a gold bridge. We laughed over this on many nights. Was it going to be worth it? It is still discussed on odd occasions, so I guess they will stay where they are. This same girl tried to earn a little spare cash by teaching English to a Dutch woman, but gave it up in desperation after a few lessons. In fact, we did hear that word had gone round the Dutch lines, "If you want to have English lessons, don't take them from an Australian!"

A black market is in full swing and a very amusing incident happened a short time ago. Nellie is Ambonese, a very dusky girl with a mop of curly black hair and dark eyes. Nellie is Number One "go-between" and dresses herself in black pyjamas for the job, so that on a dark night she just can't be seen. Night after night she walks out of the camp and does business with the natives. On this particular night she was just getting past a Jap sentry when the clock she was about to sell started its alarm ringing at top pitch. The sentry couldn't make it out and jumped round the place searching, but he didn't catch our friend, who was in fits of laughter. She went on her way and was back in camp safely before he resumed his position in the guard-box. The Japs have threatened jail and death if we continued with black-marketing, but it goes on just the same.

We have had some excellent concerts from time to time. The camp contains quite a number of talented people, mostly singers, and we have French, English, Scottish, Irish, and Dutch songs. Kong once sang to us in Chinese, but we didn't think too much of it. She giggled her way through and had us all limp with laughing. Of course we waltzed Matilda a few times. I had an amusing time when asked to join "The Barley Mow" team at a couple of concerts. Three of us dressed up as old hayseeds and each had a pretty maid on his knee, while we had to "drink to the Barley Mow in an ocean, a river, an 'ogs'ead, a gallon jar, a quart-pot, a pint-pot, a nipikin, a pipikin under the green bow". The children loved it, and were most intrigued with our coconut fibre beards, especially when the beards went up and down as we sang lustily.

Mrs Maddams could go on indefinitely doing Stanley Holloway's records word for word in the same accent, "Albert at the Zoo" and many others. She was excellent doing Noel Coward's songs, especially "Mad Dogs and Englishmen", could do a Maurice Chevalier song or two, and many other well-known songs with appropriate actions. She even made a straw boater to wear while she is being Maurice, which she also wears for water-carrying.

Of course Norah Chambers and her orchestra and the glee singers are always popular and give concerts as often as we are allowed to have them. It is a wonderful way to help pass the time. Quite often the Jap officers visit us and look in on these concerts. They always appear to appreciate them and very often send in an extra bag of rice or a little soap as a present.

17th August 1944. A lucky day for some people. We were on kitchen duty and during the morning news came that two Eurasian women with us had received the first letters from their husbands in Singapore. What a relief for them! We envied them a bit, getting a letter from home.

As the hot day wore on we were given a good ration of palm-oil, and then it fried to rain. All very important we thought then. At 4.30 p.m. Mrs Hinch and Dutch Mrs Muller (interpreter of Japanese and a very good friend of ours) walked in from the office of the guard-house next door with Rasputin. They had a large bundle of letters. Sylvia Muir and I were squatting out in the sun cleaning huge rice vats when Mrs Muller called to us, saying, "Letters for you girls."

The excitement was intense, but we didn't think we had a hope of getting one as we thought they were all from Singapore. However, we couldn't resist joining a group of our girls near by, and then Iole rushed up and told me there was one for me and none for her. The poor girl was terribly disappointed.

We had to queue up and wait for an hour, then Mrs Hinch had to sign for each letter while Rasputin sat by watching. The suspense was awful.

First letter for three years! I looked over Mrs Hinch's shoulder and suddenly saw my mother's handwriting. I went cold and goosey all over. It was so familiar, and to see it in all this awful mess and slum conditions amongst people from all the ends of the earth—it didn't seem real. I signed for it and walked away somewhere with it, and for the life of me I couldn't open it. I just stared at that handwriting. After a while Iole came along and opened it for me and I quickly read the twenty-five words in the message from home. Everything was forgotten temporarily; the whole camp life was wiped out while I read those few words. Everyone at home was well and I had two nieces! I was thrilled, for I had always wanted a niece. No war news, of course; we still have to live on what the natives tell us now that we are completely cut off from the men. We ask the natives, *"Apa kaba?"* ("What news?") The answer is always the same, "Kaba baik." ("News is good.") Could mean anything.

Three of our girls had bad news in their short letters. Loss of a parent must be a terribly hard blow to take in these circumstances. The letters have had a most peculiar effect, sadness and joy all mixed up. All the same, we feel it must be getting near the end of the war now or we wouldn't have been given them. They were two years old. A little Jap interpreter told us three months ago that three hundred letters were here for us, but we wouldn't get them till they were ready to give them to us. Oh, how we all hope they are squashed and thoroughly broken! They are a cruel, untamed, uncivilized race.

21st August 1944. Good Heavens, Seedling must be a medical orderly! Today he gave us all an injection, we think against typhoid. He was terribly fussy and did it all himself. He really gave us excellent injections. He also had us all weighed. My weight was 7 stone 3 lbs.

30th August 1944. More injections, and arms and tempers were very touchy for a few days. We all felt miserable and quite sick. If only we knew what was being injected into us! Not that we can do anything about it; we *must* have them.

Siki the Sadist came in to camp a few days ago and gave us another hour of Japanese talk, which told us, when interpreted, that we were moving back to Muntok. The civilian men apparently went there when we took this camp of theirs over last year.

What a horrible thought this trip is! It will take twenty-four hours to get there. Sixty miles of Musi River and twenty miles of Banka Strait, and no food provided. We have started buying nearly all the food we can now, mostly on the black market, so we shall have something if we are moved out suddenly.

Air-raid alerts every night now, a horrible, eerie business. We are all quiet and in bed, then suddenly cars running up and down the main road a few hundred yards away start tooting with a very sinister kind of toot. This goes on for about ten minutes, and then Jap planes fly over, giving a few bursts of machine-gun fire as a further warning. Great excitement in the guard-house and Jap houses round our camp, as they run in and out of their air-raid shelters, always carrying a rattling old tin trunk which is obviously very valuable to them. We always listen for it and remark, "There go the recipes." Our recipes are by far our most treasured possession.

We can see the Japanese procedure by gazing out of cracks,

and really, their organization of an air raid is an absolute scream. They are scared stiff, and are thickly padded all over, have cotton wool sticking out everywhere, while we poor unprotected things sit here under our shack of leaves, which would burn out in a couple of minutes! The hay-hoes stand about in shelters shivering and crying.

There have been no further alerts since the big speech, but we have been given a little extra food. Each day now we are getting fish or pork, which still comes in a soempit that moves when it is thrown to the ground outside our camp gate. It makes good stew, and that little bit of protein each day is making a big difference to our appetites. We are also allowed to write our second letter home, fifty words; we must not say we are hungry, or that we have to work so hard, or that there isn't any water, and must not mention the move to Muntok. We cannot say we are filling Fattie's tong for him each day nor can we mention how we fertilize the sweet potatoes.

10th September 1944. Rice ration has been cut and fish stopped. Our ten days' issue for five hundred people has been ten small sacks, but today only six came.

Ray is in hospital and very ill. A few days ago she was sitting on her bed-space, sewing away, when in walked Rasputin. He walked up and down the block, then suddenly screamed at Ray. There was a small notch missing in the wood boarding up the side of the hut. It was, in all probability, never there. However, he accused Ray of damaging Japanese military property and dragged her outside and made her stand in the sun. This is quite a popular punishment and most of us can stick it out, but we knew Ray couldn't. Somebody went over to her and gave her a hat to wear. Rasputin came dashing out of the guard-house at the camp entrance and threw the hat away. He smacked Ray on the face so hard he knocked her over into the sweet potato patch. Mrs Hinch went to Rasputin and begged him to allow the girl to come inside, then Dr Goldberg went from the hospital to ask him to call it off. But their entreaties were in vain. Ray had to stand there for some time, well over an hour, all of us watching her and wanting to bring her in, but we could do nothing. Eventually it happened. Ray swayed for a minute, then over she went, completely unconscious. Dr Goldberg raced out from the hospital and we dashed out from where we were. We carried her into the hospital and took not the slightest notice of Rasputin. He just stood there and stared. Ray is still desperately ill.

Much of this diary has been written in ink so far. Tweedie found a fountain pen and would always lend it to me. I could get ink from various sources round the camp and all was well. But Tweedie has been forced to sell the pen to be able to buy extra food for herself. She has had dysentery for a long time now and has lost about five stone in weight. So this will go on written in pencil.

More rice has come in, again only six sacks, but we find they contain more stones than rice. We can hardly pull ourselves across the camp these days. The Jap rations officer always weighs the rice sacks in the presence of our rations officers, but it is not until the wily Nip has left that we discover half the weight is in stones, varying in size from a walnut to a cricket ball, that are found in with the rice.

I forgot to write up our cricket match, played a few months ago for the benefit of the Dutch, who have heard so much about the game. With a worn-out tennis ball, a piece of packing case for a bat, and a kerosene tin for stumps, we went to it and had a lot of fun. We had some talent, Jess Doyle being the niece of a very well-known Australian Test player, and Iole the daughter of a former interstate bowler, so the standard should have been good. It was a terribly funny match. We had Jap guards fielding those sixers we hit over the top of the dormitories and so outside the camp. They thoroughly enjoyed themselves. Jess and Iole were the two heroines of the match, Jess top scoring and being a wizard at fielding and catching people out, like her Uncle Jack. Iole took the bowling honours, she was about the only person who could bowl *on* the wicket!

None of us think Don Bradman and company will miss anything in the way of a Test player due to our sojourn here, but we did have a most amusing day, even if we didn't impress the Dutch very much. They play a silly game like rounders in which everybody runs at once and there is a terrible muddle.

We decided to have a Test Match, England versus Australia, but somehow we have never played that Test. I'm sorry, for I'll never get another opportunity to play cricket for Australia.

Chapter 19

14th September 1944. We were asking each other how long we thought we could last on this ration, but our answer now is years and years. What a day we had yesterday! Sister James was able to make a loan for us all so we could buy sugar and extra food through the black market which still flourishes in the camp. The food comes in nearly every night by those few Indonesian hay-hoe guards who want to help us and themselves, too. Their prices are outrageous, but they are getting in sugar for us in the form of gula, also eggs, fruit, dried fish, sweet biscuits, and small moon cakes. It certainly makes life more liveable.

Tomorrow is the fifteenth, and according to the boss, Siki, we must be in Muntok, or it will be too late! Too late for what? What does he mean? We have all packed as he said. We are only allowed to take what we can carry, which has caused some heartbreaks amongst those who managed to save all their belongings. That is a grim order when one thinks of some families here, mothers with three or four children too small to carry anything. They must get all the belongings they own in the world, plus their bedding, across to Muntok under their own steam. The solution was a large auction sale.

Many people have sold many things, so clothes are getting a little more evenly distributed. Iole and I bought a man's woollen Jaeger singlet, took it to pieces, and remade it into the smartest sweater in the camp with sleeves and a navy-blue collar. It is beautifully soft and warm.

20th September 1944. We are still here! We think we shall eventually get away to Muntok, but goodness knows when.

A few days ago a truck-load of boxes arrived at the guard-house outside the camp and next door to our hut. Of course, eyes were glued to all cracks, and to our delight and joy we read "American Red Cross" in large letters on each box. Nice work, America!

The chat was superb—what would we do with milk, with tinned meat, cheese, butter, barley sugar, etc.? But we need not have worried, the good American women had worked hard for the enemy. So near to us and yet, being over the fence, how far! We saw the guards undoing boxes and boxes of medical supplies, cotton wool, dressings, bottles of medicine, jars and jars of what looked like quinine tablets. The Japs are enjoying our tinned meat and cheese and cigarettes. Even the hay-hoes are smoking our Camels and Chesterfield cigarettes. We rather hope they will choke! All we got was more dirty rice, which we now have to pick over grain by grain to remove bomb-blast, stones, glass, weevils, etc.

28th September 1944. At last the rot has stopped and black market is having the desired effect. Most of us stayed the same weight last weigh day. Think the Japs have a sense of humour after all. The food today for five hundred odd consisted of two pumpkins, twelve small gourds, and a basket of very indifferent cucumbers. When cooked it was slightly thickened pale-green water! We rescue the seeds from pumpkin when it comes and dry bake them and salt them. They make a very pleasant after-dinner savoury, as good as peanuts or almonds. Anything over and above this we have to pay for. Last week we had to pay one thousand guilders for some tapioca roots, a few coconuts, and enough brown beans to do for three meals. As Del muttered at the time, "Dear Lord, how long?"

We are going to Muntok next week. Oh, for the breath of fresh air when we get out into the sea again, after two and a half years of stifling here!

29th September 1944. All packed up and ready to go, and today we were told to unpack again. This is getting on our nerves. Better luck next time, girls.

1st October 1944. Another wow of a day. No wonder we are thin. The excitements in here, considering we have been inside four walls for so long, are terrific. There really isn't a boring moment. Early in the morning Siki arrived and called the two commandants and our black-market leaders to the guard-house. He was furious, and has put a stop to a flourishing black market. Solitary confinement in the old jail is the punishment if any more dealings with it are continued. Bang goes our supply of biscuits, eggs, gula, etc.

Later on in the morning one of our planes suddenly dived out of the clouds, then back into them a minute later. Quite a few people saw it. Next thing there was that awful ack-ack annoying us again, while the fellow pressing the button for the town siren apparently got the jitters and forgot to take his finger off. The siren went twelve times!

At 3 p.m. Rasputin arrived with more letters from all over the world. Excitement and disappointment all over again. The only one to come our way was for me. It was from a sister in the 2/7th A.G.H. Middle East, was two years old, and had come via Istanbul. We all read it and learnt that Sisters Torney and Anderson of 13th A.G.H. had been decorated with an O.B.E. and George Medal respectively. We are wondering what they did and where it happened. We were all terribly proud of them; they had been in Singapore with half of the girls here and were in the first large group to be evacuated just before the fall of Singapore. We knew they had got through to Australia.

Our families would have a fit if they could see some of our wardrobes. We are nearly all shoeless, wearing trompers until they break, then going barefooted, which is easiest of all, especially in the mud and clay. I have two pairs of shorts, a khaki pair that were old when given to me two and a half years ago, and a smart black pair made from part of a nun's gown. I also have two sun-tops, one made from the tail of Jess's shirt and the other from a nun's sleeve. Most of us are down to this. Of course, we all have a semblance of uniform left, but we are keeping that to wear home when that day comes.

I promised Iole a party if she didn't get a letter. She still has not heard from her family, and, as she says, perhaps a bomb fell on the house and killed them all at dinner, but it surely didn't kill everybody she knew. However, we had our party. We went completely haywire, and while Iole boiled a huge tin of black coffee I dashed over to a Dutch girl who sold black-market cakes to see if she had any left. She did, and we sat down to a magnificent array of four moon cakes, about as big as ping-pong balls, four baby gulas as big as a penny, and two tiny biscuits. This cost me the equivalent of fifteen shillings. We added the whole of our monthly ration of sugar, which was half a cupful, and had a feast. This is the only time we have let our heads go and it was worth it, we felt so much better for it.

3rd October 1944. Next excitement in the camp came yesterday. All the afternoon we had been watching the hay-hoes and Japs unwrapping hundreds of packets of Camel and Chesterfield cigarettes from the American Red Cross boxes we had seen arriving a couple of weeks ago, half-smoking them, then throwing them away, only to light fresh ones. To our amazement, at 5 p.m. the stuff came in here for us—what was left, anyway—to be divided between the British and Dutch. Our individual share was twenty-two cigarettes, one inch of chocolate that was growing a beard—but oh, the glorious smell of it!—half a cup of powdered milk, four tiny loaf sugars, a small packet of soup powder between three of us, a half-pound tin of jam, a small tin of meat and one of salmon for fifteen of us, an inch of cheese, a spoonful of coffee essence, and a spoonful of butter. It is only small, but it is all wonderful, be it ever so old. Thank you very much, America.

For tea last night we had a thin piece of tinned meat one inch long. The taste and smallness of these things does terrible things to us. Really, we don't know whether it is better to go without that small taste or not, as it is so more-ish. Today for lunch we had a teaspoonful of salmon with our rice. It was glorious and flavoured the whole of the rice. We had already had a king's breakfast with real milk on our rice porridge. We now realize how bitter soya-bean milk is. We also had our jam ration, a teaspoonful. How different it tasted from the brew we make here out of cast off lime-skins, which we call marmalade, or the jam we make from banana skins, which is like eating stewed shoelaces, or tamarind, which we call dried apricot jam!

A rumour went round with the American food that the war with Germany is almost finished and that the Allies are fighting on German soil at last. We are once more having daily alerts, but nothing much happens other than that sinister car-tooting in the distance nearly every night.

Yesterday three truck-loads of heavy sacks of rice arrived, and we had to send out squads to unload them and carry them into an old garage near by. We always have to unload and carry in our own rice, but never before have we been asked to unload and store at least two hundred huge sacks of rice while the Japs sat round and smoked our cigarettes. When the women could hardly stagger on their feet the Japs called it off and gave them a "present" of a couple of tins of pâté de fois gras. Rather ironical, when it was taken from our own Red Cross boxes! We often wonder how much of the Red Cross stuff they removed for themselves before letting us get at it. We know they have had dozens of tins of cheese, butter, milk, and thousands of peppermints, as their cooks, who are Indonesians from this camp and go in to work for them daily, have told us. The cooks said they have kept back thousands of cigarettes.

4th October 1944. A dentist came today, and for the first time actually did some work. He usually comes, has a look at one or two patients, then says, *"Nanti, nanti"* ("Wait"), and disappears. He did quite a lot of work today, removing teeth without any anaesthetic. As each person emerged she looked terrible and was usually in tears as well as in agony. One of our girls had a tooth out. He broke off her tooth and then chiselled the rest of it out until she couldn't stand any more. She was in such pain that she walked over to the Dutch lines instead of to her own block and for a while didn't seem to know where she was. Roasting in hell is far too delicate a punishment for these brutes.

A couple of hours after the dentist left all his victims were made to stand outside the guard-house, while drunken Ah Fat gave them a lecture for over an hour because only one person had said thank you to the dentist.

Here are some of our recipes:

Milk. Soak soya beans overnight, skin them, pound them, put in a cooking tin, then add some water, well covering them. Bring almost to the boil then drain off.

Cheese. Keep some soya-bean milk overnight; in the morning it is sour. Add salt, pepper, and tie it in an old piece of loosely woven rag. Hang on a nail for two days and it turns into soft cheese.

Anchovy Paste. Gather everybody's left-over fish-bones, wash and dry them. Dry-bake them on a piece of tin, pound them while still hot, add salt, pepper, juice of a lime if there is one about, stir in a little red palm-oil to make a paste, and there it is, anchovy paste!

Potato Chips. Finely cut cucumber skins and banana skins, then fry in a little oil until crisp. Sprinkle with salt.

Marmalade Steam Pudding. After removing all weevils, mix gaplek flour and cooked rice, pinch of salt, and enough water to make a dough. Cut some lime-skin very finely and put it in the bottom of a bully-beef tin, add a little gula and water to this, then fill the tin with dough. Steam for half an hour, blowing at the fire the whole way. Result? A perfect little two-by-two-inch steam pudding with marmalade running down its sides.

Seasoned Duckling. This can only be done if there is any black-market green gram available. Boil green gram until soft. Pound curry stuffs together, chilli, saffron, ginger (all home-grown), onion, one clove, and a small piece of cinnamon bark. When well pounded and blended, fry in a little red palm-oil, then add cooked green gram and stir well until curry stuffs well into the gram. Serve with rice, shut your eyes, and it could be seasoned duckling. Really!

Chapter 20

15th October 1944. At last we have moved back to Muntok. We are now retracing our steps—only Singapore, and then we are back where we started.

It was our cooking day on Wednesday, 5th October. We were having our lunch when we were told to be ready in two hours to go with an advance party of forty British as "kitchen staff". It was the first split of our thirty-two sisters. We wanted to keep together and move together, but we did not have any say in the matter. Eight of us had to go with this first group.

There was quite an upheaval and much fussing about the place and everything seemed to be one large muddle. After leaving our most important things behind us, and waiting as usual for ship transport, we finally left at 6.15 p.m. as darkness descended.

We were driven once more, packed like sardines in an

K

open truck with a shocking driver, down to the wharf some miles away. Our "ship" was much better than we expected. It was a three-decker river boat, once used on the Penang-Malaya mainland trip by the British before the war. We had the middle deck, and what a relief to be able to walk around and lie on a clean floor! At 8 p.m. we moved across the river to a station called something like Kertaputi, to pick up one hundred and twenty more internees from a place called Benkoelen, on the other side of Sumatra. There were about a dozen or so Dutch nuns in the party, the remainder being Indonesians and Indo-Dutch.

Our luggage consisted of what we could carry; their luggage consisted of all their worldly possessions. Soon after we had settled once more on our piece of deck the Japs made ten of us go ashore and carry all this luggage on board. It took us until midnight to get it on, and it nearly killed us. We have never lifted anything so heavy, some of it we couldn't raise from the ground, so we had to drag it on board. It felt like lead. To think of what we left behind, and now we had to burst our boilers carrying heavy stuff for Indonesians who had been travelling all day! When we stopped for a rest, or when it got too heavy to even drag it, Jap officers would make us do it by flashing their swords very close to our arms and legs, far too close to disregard, in fact we had to skip aside smartly to miss the sword. We now know that luggage contained china, silver, books, chairs, rice, cabin trunks of more rice and corn, heavy stone pounders, and Heaven knows what else.

The only pleasant interlude was when I stole two huge fat bananas from a Jap guard's bicycle—he saw me and was so staggered he didn't stop me.

When all this stuff was on board and Sister Catherinia had missed the plank gangway and fallen in the river, we went back to our spot on board for a rest. Not so. Along came these brutes screaming for us and hitting us on the legs with their swords, and took us off to the station, where we had to unload a railway truck full of rice and put that on board, too. Then on went dozens of coffins, a gruesome sight at that hour of the morning. Two of the girls found a sack of sugar and poked a hole in it, and we all filled our pockets.

We stopped work at about two or three a.m., then could only sleep in turns, since we had to keep our own guard on our precious few belongings; the crew was on the prowl.

This heavy luggage-carrying was my Waterloo as a useful member of the community. While dragging one of those heavy trunks I suddenly developed a shocking pain under my ribs, and have been in agonies ever since, as well as having diarrhoea.

In the meantime, back at our camp, cooks had been working all night with the aid of the Snake—the only time he has been helpful—cooking fried rice cakes, frying small pieces of pork, and making tea for us. This was brought down to us next morning, and was to do us until we arrived at our destination.

When we woke in the morning we were so stiff and sore and tired we could hardly move. When the Snake arrived with tea and food we fell to and had quite a good breakfast, leaving half of the food to have later in the day. Except for two buckets of tea, there was no water at all on board.

We relaxed all day while we went down that sixty sticky miles of river, and the relief at 2 p.m. to be out of the hot river and suddenly to smell the sea and breathe in fresh sea air was marvellous and stimulating. We passed close to the spot where we lost *Vyner Brooke* and twelve of our sisters were drowned in February 1942.

We anchored a mile off Muntok pier late that afternoon, but were not transhipped until it was quite dark and rough and stormy. Forty of us then had a nightmare journey in a dirty Japanese junk thing. None of the new-comers would come; they stayed on board. We entered a tiny hole in the roof, then came down a few steps and had to jump the rest of the way to the bottom into two inches of kerosene. What a smell! We had to sit and soak in this. Our luggage was thrown at us by half a dozen Japs who were constantly screaming at the top of their voices. Nearly all of us were sick, and just as we left the bigger vessel an air-raid siren screamed. The Japs screamed more, put out their torches and closed the trap over that tiny hole, leaving us in pitch blackness. We tossed and tipped in the black, foul hell-hole for some considerable time, until at last we bumped into something solid. The trapdoor was opened and we saw to our horror that we were back against the ship we had left. We stayed for a while, then the trapdoor was shut once more and away we went tossing again.

When we finally reached the pier we were all so ill we didn't care or worry about belongings. We were so weak we couldn't get out and Japanese soldiers had to come and half lift us up on to the pier. Last time we arrived at Banka Island we were dressed only in a working army uniform. This time, we landed as we did last time, wet, cold, hungry, ill, with no luggage, though this time we did have a hat each. We didn't care if we never saw our belongings again. We stumbled down that long pier, quite a few of the women fainting on the way; it was grim, but the fresh air helped us to recover quickly.

The Japs had provided lorries for nearly two hundred people, but as only forty came ashore we actually relaxed with ten to each truck. It took us some time to get to the end of the pier and reach the trucks.

Just before we moved off our belongings were thrown in to us; we hadn't expected to see them again. I had my diary and drawings in their precious bundle tied round my waist, could not risk their being left round the place in a Japanese junk.

We had a very pleasant drive that night in the open trucks along a coconut-palm-lined roadway. This drive stimulated us and our sense of humour returned. Fortunately we were in the last truck, which lost the rest of the convoy, and we went for a perfectly glorious drive for miles before our driver realized he was lost. We went back and eventually arrived in the new camp.

Everything was huge and brand-new and spotless. There was lots of room and bed-space, each person had a new rush mat to sleep on, with at least a yard of space on either side before meeting the next person—such a change after being cramped into 20½ inches to rest on.

The men were camped in the old original coolie lines we first lived in, and they sent over so much food we couldn't cope with it all. Rice porridge cooked in coconut milk, buckets of rice, vegetables, and fried salt fish, with gallons of tea arrived for us. After eating all we could we filled everything we owned with cooked rice so we could dry it in the sun next day and store it away for our next rainy day. We all slept soundly that night.

Daylight inspection showed the new camp to be on top of a rise, so we could get a breath of fresh sea air every now and then. It was built on a gravel surface, no mud or clay here. But it was a very jerry-built affair; it was tied together, no nails anywhere. There were six big huts, each capable of housing one hundred and forty people, three huge kitchens, one main kitchen in the middle of the camp, the other two, containing about fifty small concrete fireplaces each, were two huts away from the main kitchen and quite well spaced out in the camp. The thing that worried us was that the lavatories, cement pits only, were right alongside the kitchens. The community bathrooms, cement-floored and boarded up by attap only, were next door to the lavatories.

We found we had nine wells, cemented and clean this time, but the water was at least fifty feet down and soon ran out once we started on it. All wells were empty within twenty-four hours, so we were taken to a tiny creek about ten minutes' walk through pretty jungle and past wildflowers down into a tiny gully. It all seems very promising so far.

We have to do heavy work sinking posts and putting a barbed-wire fence round the hospital, and carrying sacks of rice, wood, and so on, but we are allowed to go to the creek and bathe and do our washing if we have been on a working squad. The first day I went in a small water-carrying squad at 6 a.m. and it was perfect. We all remarked that it was good to be alive.

We won't have to worry about wood for a while. The three kitchens have a high wall round them outside, consisting of chopped wood. Wonders will never cease! Taratani, our new boss, ordered us to carry the wood to an empty hut at the other end of the camp, as far away from the kitchen as possible. Then, a few days later, it had to be carried back to its original place beside the kitchen. Perverse devils, but it did mean another trip to the creek for a bathe.

The day after we arrived the remaining people from our river steamer came and spread themselves out over the new huts and allowed us to cook for them. Food was better for us for a while until the second group came from Palembang. They were all Dutch. We had a wonderful meal ready for them when they arrived late one night, cold and hungry. We were able to give them fresh green vegetables, fried fish and rice, and plenty of tea. They did enjoy it.

We started to get quite a good ration of "fresh" fish. It was obviously caught in nets early in the morning and left to the flies and the sun on the sand until mid-afternoon, then brought in to us. They were tiny fish, so the answer was to wash them, then deep-fry them whole. They crisped beautifully and we ate them like biscuits, heads, insides, bones, just one or two crisp bites and they were gone. Think of the calcium!

One afternoon they brought in a huge stingray. An Indonesian told us it would be good fried, but we didn't have any more oil, so we sent our acting commandant, Mrs Maddams, to ask the new rations officer, a weak-looking individual, for some palm-oil to use for cooking the fish. Unheard of cheek on our part, but it acted and he staggered in with a kerosene tin full.

After working squads had dissected that huge stingray into small pieces our cooking squad deep-fried it. It was the nicest fish we have tasted. Wilma, Iole, Vivian, and I were cooking squad that day and we didn't finish cooking until about 8 p.m.

A few days later we had a whole shark, which was nearly as good.

Two weeks after our arrival the remainder of the British arrived on a dark night, and what a tale they told! It was a relief to see the rest of our sisters with them, but they had all had a foul twenty-four hours without any food and only the water they carried. They travelled in an awful Jap coolie boat thing, no room even to lie down and had to sit huddled together the whole time. The Japs didn't even produce a lavatory.

They looked terrible when they finally drew up in trucks, standing up clutching each other. Most of them were too weak to get down. Wilma and Vivian jumped into the trucks and helped them down while we others were trying to cope with those who fainted after they got out. They were cold, hungry, and utterly worn out, a nightmare of a trip for the older women amongst them.

We knew they were coming and had the usual feast of rice, vegetables, fried shark, and gallons of tea and coffee ready for them. Just as we started to give out this food, in walked the world's champion sadist, Siki. Nobody invited him to Banka Island! He took one look at the food and another at these weary, hungry people and ordered, 'No food tonight.' They were allowed to have the tea or coffee only. Siki put guards on the kitchen and the food all night and would not let anyone into the kitchen until the morning. The food must have been awful then, but they ate it.

How those Japs hate the British! That suits us; we must be giving them merry hell somewhere.

Chapter 21

10th November 1944. Have been in hospital here for some time with a mixed infection of Banka fever and my initial dose of malaria. Suddenly felt very ill one morning and was carried over here to the hospital, hoping somebody could remove my head; it felt as if it were about to burst. In a week I was joined by Mitz, Shirley Gardham, Mickey Syer, and Jennie Greer, all with this awful fever, raging temperatures, and unconsciousness, followed by skin actions. It is such a mixture of things that for want of a better name the doctors have called it "Banka fever".

Mickey had just arrived with the last group from Palembang, mainly hospital patients and staff. They, too, had an awful nightmare of a trip, being forced to sit shoulder to shoulder on a small low craft only three feet above the water. Those on the outside could keep themselves cool by dangling their feet in the water. During the night at sea they ran into a storm and tossed and turned. Not one of them thought they would ever survive it, for the boat was completely out of control. Patients have told me that Mickey was wonderful and moved about amongst the sick all night long doing what she could for them. She is a grand girl. Incidentally she has the loveliest soft singing voice and has often sung pretty little songs for us at night when the day's work was done.

Ray is better and has been discharged from hospital, but must not do anything strenuous.

The camp hospital is much bigger and better organized here. We have a ward taking about nineteen patients lying alongside each other on the "bali bali". This is a long shelf affair about two feet off the floor and made from thin branches of rubber-trees bound together. It sways and creaks when anyone turns over. The children's ward takes four patients on the bali bali, and there are also two old cots; one cot can take two babies. The infectious block consists of four small rooms taking three patients each on the bali bali, with enough room for one sister only to be able to turn and come out after doing her work. Fifty yards away is the convalescent hospital, which is bigger and has much more room and fresh air. This takes about thirty patients and is actually a part of one of the big blocks of the main camp.

Our four doctors are now working very hard among our internees, because the place is so much bigger. We now number over seven hundred. One doctor looks after the hospital, another is in charge of convalescent and the daily clinic, while the other two are flat out looking after the six blocks in the camp. Since we have started to get so much fever they are kept on the run.

The nursing staff is now getting properly organized; it is all hands to the pump to cope with the increasing sickness and fever. The Dutch Charitas nuns continued to staff the hospital as they have done from the beginning, but they needed more assistance, so we Australians have been released from our camp chores to give more time to nursing. We were not allowed to nurse in the hospital before this. Now good cooks, vegetable-cutters, water-carriers, and wood-choppers are nurses again and on a daily roster of hospital or "district" nursing in the blocks.

The English and Australian sisters got together once more and decided to divide into these two groups, hospital staff and district nurses. This was the only way to cope with this dreadful fever that has hit the camp. It recurs every few weeks and nothing seems to stop it.

The Dutch civilian nurses have stopped nursing; only one has continued, and there are many of them among the five hundred Dutch people now interned with us. The only nursing staff now are the Dutch nuns and the British nurses. Sister Reynelda, a nun, and our Sister Jean Ashton now act as joint matrons in the hospital. Another Charitas nun has done an amazing job boiling an oil-drum of the hospital and sick people's washing every day from the day she was interned in April 1942. She now washes for at least forty or fifty people every day. We say she is obviously being fed meat or she couldn't stand up to it! There is no doubt about it, women *are* cats.

Another nun, Sister Cecile, cooks special things and makes hot drinks for the sickest of the hospital patients as well as cooking for all the nuns, and has worked over a fire every day and all day since 1942. We all admire the strength of these nuns; they can last much longer on duty than we can, but then they don't have to come off duty and earn a living as we do, as well as doing other chores.

We are doing everything within our power for every sick person. Nippon could help if he would bring in medicines and quinine, but all he does is to bring in a small bottle of one hundred quinine tablets for seven hundred people once every five or six weeks—practically useless.

When patients are admitted to hospital they bring their own bedding, if any, because the bali bali is so uneven to lie on. We nearly all own a rice-sack "mattress" now and cover ourselves as best we can. Now we are thin we get cold at night.

When nursing we have to walk along the bali bali, stepping

between patients, and find many death-traps, for the binding of the branches forming the bed-space often breaks and down we go between the slats, often falling over the patients and always taking the skin off our already thin legs. Not the best conditions for nursing! Night duty is a nightmare; there is only one oil lamp and plenty of bunkers to fall into on the way while doing a round of the hospital.

At the moment there are nine of our girls in hospital and two very ill in the blocks. All have Banka fever. There are at least thirty people sick in each block and things are grim. We hope it will soon subside, and then all will be well, for this is a much cooler and cleaner camp and surely must be more healthy for us. There is a pleasant sea breeze all day and we are high up and well out of any swamps. Water is the main problem; the wells can't cope. There isn't much lighting either, only one oil lamp to each block of a hundred and forty people. This is very hard on mothers who have young children to look after.

The latest Nipponese idea is that we do night duty in the camp instead of the guards. One person has to be on duty in each block "in case of fire". How the mosquitoes worry the people on night duty! It isn't so bad if you own slacks, but it is wicked being out amongst the mosquitoes in shorts all night long. Every now and then a Jap comes in to do a round to see if there *is* somebody on guard duty, and what a fuss and noise when he finds that tired-out person asleep in an old chair outside her block!

Now and again during the night an agonizing scream is heard; it means some poor soul has fallen through the slats and into the lavatory. As this is a concrete pit about five feet deep, with the level only a few inches from the top, it is an awful business getting her out and clean again. This surely must be the worst thing that can happen in anybody's life! Unfortunately, the drains run into the lavatories, which does not help matters.

18th November 1944. We don't think we'll be home for Christmas after all. I am still in hospital and getting malaria,

143

but have been transferred to convalescent. This is much better. If only I could get out of here and help my friends a bit! Iole looks awful; she has just finished a week of night duty and has both arms and legs bandaged to protect infected mosquito bites. Iole said it was the stiffest week of night duty she has ever done. Three Englishwomen died during that time. Today two more British women are unconscious and two hundred and ten are down with this peculiar fever in the blocks, most of them British. Why are we getting it more than the Dutch? We are certainly much thinner.

22nd November 1944. Three more young Englishwomen died today and we are all hoping and praying they will be the last. This is getting too awful; this epidemic must be stopped.

There is no contact whatever with the men in the jail; we often wonder if this fever is in their camp, too.

When people die the women have to carry them out of the camp to a small Chinese cemetery in the jungle not far from here. We have a special corner for the people from this camp. Our working squads have to dig the graves with chungkals; spades would help a lot if we had some. The missionaries or the nuns always take the service at the graveside. The cemetery is in a very pretty spot on the hillside, with a profusion of wild jungle flowers everywhere. The two commandants have insisted on small wooden crosses being given by the Japanese to mark the graves and the inscriptions are burnt on them. Norah Chambers and Mrs Owen do this work beautifully.

Our old ration truck has arrived from Palembang, plus Tanaka, the driver, plus the old weighing-in scales. Tanaka is a fairly reasonable fellow and we were rather relieved to see him. He did his best to bring extra rations during those last few months in the "men's" camp in Palembang. We laughed when we saw the old scales arriving. In spite of rumours, this looks horribly like permanent residence here. Should not be; we have "done" nearly three years.

The Reverend Mother Laurentia is the Dutch commandant and is a wonderful person. Very tall, upright, and altogether a fine person, she has a rather limited supply of English, but quite enough to make herself understood. She had denied herself anything others could not have, and although she grows thinner and thinner as the years go on she never loses her beautiful smile, and always handles her problems from a very practical view point. We are fortunate to have such fine women as the two commandants, Mother Laurentia and our Mrs Hinch.

A week ago Mother Laurentia came into hospital and told us we had been given some money, which came from the same source as the American Red Cross food we had received a few months ago.

That is one of the things that amazes us about the Japs. They appear to be quite honest about internees' money, and have, on many occasions, brought money from husbands in Singapore to their wives in this camp. Now this large sum has arrived and it works out at eleven guilders each. What a relief this is! Hospital and camp expenses are terrific; we pay 50 cents for a green mango and 60 cents for an indifferent banana. Jap rations alone would not keep anyone alive.

In one week the Japs have skinned most of us of that money in exchange for oil, sugar, coffee, beans, and a little fruit. It was good while it lasted, but the Japs soon collected it again.

I don't appear to be frantically strong after all, for this morning I was helping to give out the convalescent patients' breakfast bowls of rice porridge and dropped a whole trayful of the precious porridge on the dirty ground, and some into a bucket of water, equally precious. Simply couldn't hold it. I felt awful, because there would not be any left over in the main kitchen. Fortunately some kind soul produced enough from the main hospital building to make up for the loss. I was put back to bed at once by Dr McDowell and it was three hours before my heart stopped thumping. Quite my worst moment in camp so far, dropping patients' precious food.

27th November 1944. Still here in hospital. All weighed today; all lost weight. Iole is 7 stone, and I couldn't go more than 6 stone 12 pounds—all caused by this wretched fever.

145

We hear that the British are going to be moved to Singapore, but we don't believe all we hear about moves now.

Today some beans and salt fish came in at an awful price. Iole and I were flat broke, so Iole dashed off and sold the shorts she sleeps in so we could buy this food. We bought it and have five guilders left over!

8th December 1944. Sold a zip-fastener from an old blouse plus our ration of Chesterfield cigarettes, which we had kept for such an emergency. We were given one guilder each for the cigarettes. Thank goodness we only smoked one each when we got them, thinking they might be useful some day!

It is three years today since this war started, and I notice we are sitting behind a Jap flag flying gaily over the entrance. How we hate that infernal red blob! They are so proud of what they did at Pearl Harbour. We all hope we don't celebrate their fourth anniversary with them. Surely not?

9th December 1944. Out of hospital at last; now I can go on the nursing staff. Six weeks of lying and sitting on the thinnest spine, always on a community bed alongside fifteen other people who are sick, is not much fun. The bali bali is most uncomfortable and sticks into us at odd places, not adding to our comfort. As I left hospital two more Australian sisters were admitted.

28th December 1944. Couldn't write about this period; it has been too awful, one or two funerals every day and so many young people are dying.

There are funeral squads now, the stronger women having to go to the cemetery and make the graves, still using chungkals only. The young boys of the camp are now helping the Japs make the coffins and they have to carry them to the hospital when needed. Goodness knows what it must do to them.

Funerals are arranged by the internees and we carry the coffin out to the cemetery, always escorted by a Jap guard. He usually allows us to detour a little and pick some wildflowers.

Our first Christmas as prisoners we dined in English style, having steak and onions sent by our men; our second Christmas, which we hoped would be the last, was Malay style eating mah mee for Christmas dinner. We were so sure we were brought over here to Banka Island for repatriation that our third Christmas hit us rather suddenly, and we were forced to have it Chinese style, fried rice with fried oddments through it. These oddments were a little piece of pork, half a garfish, and a few prawns, so we really had a feast. The Japs gave us two tiny pigs and a small sack of rice for "being good". When the pigs were prepared and ready to be cooked a guard walked into the kitchen, cut off the hind legs, and walked off with them. So that was that. We had the rest.

There were no presents for each other this year; we simply have not got a thing, not even paper to make Christmas cards. Iole gave me the Christmas card I made and gave to her two years ago. I gave her some flowers sitting in a tiny shell I found by the fence. Iole has just recovered from her first attack of malaria, all but two sisters have had it now. Routine is to lie on our bed-space and keep covered with anything we can lay hands on and stay put until the attack wears off. It quite often takes some days. This one quinine tablet now and then is hopeless.

9th January 1945. Weighed today, 6 stone 7 pounds, now lighter than Iole, who is 7 stone. Everybody in camp has lost weight this time. Nearly three years of this slimming and slumming now. Today our lords and masters had the nerve to ask for a squad of *strong women* to go and dig more graves outside, stressing the point, "not the same ones". Quite a point, too, since the wealthy are the strong and they don't do the work; they pay others to do it for them, hence "the same ones". However, it is extraordinary how a person can have malaria and a temperature of over 104° every week or so and yet be able to work in between bouts of it.

We are being fed now on rice and jack fruit. This is a horrible-tasting wild jungle fruit; natives won't eat it more than once a week. We get it every day and it is loathsome, quite often makes us vomit. We are now getting four teaspoons of sugar and salt once every fourteen days; I am afraid there are not too many "willing women" left!

23rd January 1945. Thirty-one of our thirty-two sisters now have malaria quite badly, and we are all so tired we are hoping and praying for our freedom. If it doesn't happen soon we shall all be messes for the rest of our lives. You can't treat tropical fevers, ulcers, etc., on this diet and lack of water; it just won't work.

There have been many more deaths; there are no old people left in camp now. We have six of our girls in hospital, four of them very ill, Ray, Blanche Hempsted, Shirley Gardham, and Rene Singleton. We are all doing everything we can for them, "specialing" them day and night when they have their bad moments.

Iole, Vivian, Wilma, and Jean Ashton are earning their living being nightmen. They get eighty cents a day from a camp pooled supply of money to do this filthy job. Because of the drains running into the lavatories and no "fertilizing", thank God, going on here, things became rather desperate and something had to be done. The original sanitary squad, who carried on in this camp from our last camp, simply could not cope. So these girls get up at the crack of dawn and work.

Their tools of trade, provided by the Japanese, are two kerosene tins, two half coconut shells nailed on sticks for scoops, and a long pole to help carry the tin away—completely and utterly inadequate for the job. They have to walk a good half-mile each trip, six trips before breakfast. They have to take it out of the camp and away quite a distance into the jungle on the other side of the main road running past the camp entrance. These girls are tops; they chat away to each other as they walk past our block "carrying", as they call it, and it is always about something quite pleasant, never a grumble. They even work double time so the pay won't be lost if one of them goes down with fever. Wish I could help them, am back in bed again and down to six stone.

Yesterday letters arrived again from all over the world, most of them through the Vatican this time. Jess Doyle and Flo Trotter seem to be the luckiest of our girls, they hardly ever miss. The Dutch people have had about five mails in these three years, mostly from Java, Celebes, etc. Our people have had a few odd ones from Singapore. Poor little Iole still hasn't heard from her family. We often think of those mothers who haven't heard from their daughters and still don't know they are not here with the rest of us. They must be nearly demented with worry.

Funnily enough, all the news contained in mail from overseas seems to give us the impression there is peace everywhere but here on Banka Island. According to letters from Australia, they are not worried about war now and people's families write of their *holidays*! The sentence "peace and plenty" comes in a letter from Scotland to a Scots nurse here with us; missionaries are working in South China. It has got us all wondering. . . .

We saw our first coconuts for months today. They came into camp at just under three dollars—used to be seven cents in 1942.

26th January 1945. Vivian and Iole have had an accident carrying. Something slipped, they both juggled with the long pole they carry on their shoulders, one behind the other, Iole missed it and it poked her in the chest heavily. As the pain didn't die down at all she reported to the doctor, who has bandaged a fractured rib. This is the first fracture we have had in camp. Just as well, we could do little with fractured arms and legs, and as for surgery, if anybody needed immediate surgery she would have to go without; there is no equipment here at all.

7th February 1945. The camp is full of desperately ill women with beriberi and Banka fever; it is not letting up at all.

Our monthly pay arrived yesterday, many months overdue. It was given to us at 9 a.m. At 10 a.m. the Japs had most of it back again for rations received. Why do they go to the trouble of paying us? Saving face, if any? It makes an awful lot of work for those people giving it out, then collecting it again an hour or so later.

8th February 1945. Our own Ray, Sister Raymont, died today after thirty-six hours of being desperately ill. Ray had an attack of malaria, suddenly became unconscious, and didn't recover. We are all absolutely rocked. Ray has never really recovered properly since that damned Jap made her stand in the sun for so long a few months ago, just because a small knot in the wood on the wall behind her bed-space had fallen out. Val Smith has lost her best friend.

Our girls gave Ray a military funeral, all wearing their uniforms. It made the Japs sit up; they even stood to attention and removed their caps as it went past their quarters, a thing they had never done before.

17th February 1945. Am back in hospital again, this time alongside Kong, who is recovering from malaria and overwork. Today she produced some Pond's Vanishing Cream from Heaven knows where and let me have a little of it. The first face cream for three years! My skin seems gloriously soft at the moment. It seemed to have an almost overpowering perfume. We have noticed that if anybody wears face powder we can smell her coming long before she reaches us. Heavens, we must have come down to earth!

If I give Kong a banana skin and some chilli she chops away as she chats away, squatting on her bed-space, and mutters to me about "hellfire sambal", which she gets cooked and we have on our rice. The banana skin is quite unrecognizable!

Our Vi McElnea and Mavis Hannah are doing a grand job for hospital patients. It is the rainy season and quite cold at times, so these two sisters are frying up all patients' rice at midday and evening meals. They charge ten cents so they can buy extra food for themselves when it comes in; they both look as if they need it! It is quite a job, for they have to wangle their way outside the camp to get sticks and bits and pieces of wood to keep their fire going. They never charge our own girls to hot up their food because they say "you are in the family".

Pat Blake is in hospital, too, and is on the bali bali opposite me. She and I have long chats at night about recipes and how to cook different things. Pat has promised to make me an

Irish stew if I visit her in Sydney, and let me have some cold next day with fresh bread and butter, on condition that I give her a chocolate meringue pudding with cream when she visits me in Melbourne.

Being nurses as well as patients, we work quite hard—silly, really. We have to do night duty in turns and we are kept going pretty hard all night, then in the daytime I have to help with the convalescent patients' rations and deal out the food. Have far less work to do when not a patient.

20th February 1945. Dear old Rene Singleton died today of beriberi after being in hospital for some weeks. We are all terribly sad; everyone liked Rene so much, she was always the life of the party at our worst moments. She was in her early thirties.

20th March 1945. Find it very hard to write these days as there is nothing pleasant to write about. Camp life is just an existence now. No more concerts or charades or sing-songs; when the day's work is done people go off to their beds and lie there until morning.

We are going back to Sumatra. Thank God we are going to get away from this camp! We all thought we would be right in this new, large camp, but it is mainly the lack of water that has started this terrible illness here. The tiny creek the water comes from is surely filthy now and full of wogs, and there is well water only after rain. The mud and heat and mosquitoes of Palembang are preferable to this. We are told Banka Island is known as Dead Man's Island.

Sister Blanche Hempsted of Queensland, died yesterday—malnutrition and beriberi once more. Blanche had been very ill in hospital for some time. In the end she must have known she would not get well, because she apologized to one of her friends who was sitting there with her for taking so long to die. She died half an hour later.

We now number only twenty-nine. Everybody is blaming the white rice we were getting for all this beriberi. When we used to get a little red rice on odd occasions things were much better. We are told there is no nourishment in white rice.

We are not going to Palembang after all. Our famous or infamous Mr Siki has spoken again. He tells us we are going to a place called Loebok (or Lubuck) Linggau, which is on the far side of Sumatra from here, in other words, on the southern side. We go back across the Banka Strait, sixty miles up that hateful river to Palembang, then train across Sumatra, and finally trucks. The camp is on a rubber estate; there should be plenty of shade there, this yellow gravel is very glaring and hard on our eyes. Siki promises plenty of meat in the way of deer, wild boar, etc., and red rice.

The trip, we are told, will take three days. Won't that be fun, travelling *à la* Nipponese with all these sick people! So far we have had sixty-one deaths in the short time we have been here.

We were told we should go on the 20th March, that is, today, and there is no sign of a move, more a sign of permanency. An old battered piano and some chairs arrived a few days ago, also six goats, a few fowls, and some pigs. We wondered why, but now we know. A very important Jap official is coming for an inspection, bringing Red Cross goods for us. They tell us he is from the office of the Foreign Minister; that sounds most impressive!

For two days the place was stripped of weeds, small bridges were put over gutters, and the hospital was "scrubbed and polished". The day he arrived Flo Trotter put on her uniform and borrowed a veil from someone and was on duty in the hospital, looking very chic for an internee, and quite ready to make a good impression. At last, with a flourish of car tooters, about nine huge cars arrived in camp. Out stepped this fellow and sixteen friends. They walked straight to the far end of the camp and back, taking bows from the women and children of each block as they passed them. These people had been standing at tenko for almost an hour waiting for his arrival. The Japanese then climbed into their cars and departed. They didn't go inside the blocks, didn't sight the hospital or the goats (same thing) or the piano or the little bridges. The whole inspection took about ten minutes!

The message he brought all the way from Tokyo was, "My kind regards to the women and children and I'll give them a present when they get to their new camp"—condescending devil! They love treating us as kids. No doubt his present has been sent to us from America. He said he would send Red Cross goods to the new camp and save us carrying them!

Within an hour or so of his departure the piano, chairs, pigs, and fowls were taken away again. The goats were not worth removing.

Iole is O.C. goats because in a weak moment she said she loved them! She takes them round the camp for a bit of a browse, leading them on bits and pieces of rope and string and rag. She even tries to milk the miserable specimens when they look a bit in need of it. They are very scrawny-looking beasts; one dropped dead soon after arrival. My friend was most upset. From a distance she looks as if she is taking her large dogs for an airing.

Little Dutch Bill Wenning, who was born in camp nearly three years ago, asked his mummy why the "goots" had one tail in front and one tail behind! He is most intrigued and follows Iole and her goats everywhere. He has never seen any animals other than a few dogs and the old bullock that sometimes brings the rations. All the small children call this bullock "Gho Leng", and if they see a picture of a bullock in a book, they call it a Gho Leng, after the Chinese who used to bring fruit into the camp in his bullock cart way back in 1942. What a surprise is in store for these children who were born in camp, or came in as babes, when they see trains, ships, beaches, real toys, tricycles and toy motor cars, doll's houses, people riding horses—even when they see white men! Half of them haven't a clue what their fathers look like. Suppose they expect something short and yellow with black stiff hair and slit eyes.

4th April 1945. Our Shirley Gardham, from Tasmania, collapsed and died this afternoon in hospital. It was very sudden, a matter of minutes only. It has knocked us all sideways. As Shirley always loved flowers so much the girls are busy arranging some beautiful wildflowers for her now.

8th April 1945. The first group from our camp has left for Sumatra. One third of the people took off this morning, packed as usual, in trucks. We hope they have a good trip; it is a tough one this time. Half of our sisters have gone with them. We hate being separated like this, even if it is only temporarily.

Chapter 22

20th April 1945. On 12th April the second group of prisoners started off in the rain on the three days trek to Loebok Linggau. This group consisted of hospital patients and about one hundred other people. Those remaining in camp were to follow us in about four days' time.

What a business! About six people were desperately ill, some of them unconscious, and in spite of the doctors' begging the Japs to allow them to remain until the last party left they had to travel that day. They obviously had only a few hours to live, and it seemed criminal to move them.

We were told to be ready at 6 a.m., so we all dined on hard cold rice cooked the night before, which stuck in our throats, and waited until 11 a.m. before we left in the pouring rain in open trucks. What a way to transport sick people!

We were driven at break-neck speed to the pier, and there the stretcher patients were unloaded and put on the grass beneath trees, the only shelter from the rain. It was ghastly. One Dutch woman died there..

Those who could walk started off carrying their own baggage as best they could, along that long, long pier, resting every few yards. Half a dozen of our sisters were stretcher-bearers and walked that pier many times, carrying and helping those too ill to walk. How they kept it up nobody knows.

We all noticed a big difference in the pier this time. There were camouflaged gun emplacements every few yards and dozens of armed Japs everywhere. But they didn't help us; they only stared with an expression of horror on their faces at the pitiful, long, strung-out file of weary and terribly ill people.

After some hours everybody was at last at the end of the pier, where we were all helped into a small launch by Sister James and Iole, the two smallest amongst our group of sisters. They also managed to get the stretcher patients aboard this awkward, bumping little launch without dropping them in the water. When the launch was full it went off tossing and bumping about until it came alongside an old wooden hulk of a thing, like a small coastal cargo vessel. So this was the "big boat" Siki promised us? He apparently doesn't know much about ships!

As Pat Blake and I were walking patients we were made to go down into the hatch and squat on crawling rice sacks with so many other women and children and babes that it was impossible for anyone to stretch her legs. And hot! It was like a furnace. The thought of twenty-four hours of that didn't help matters, especially as we both had dysentery, and we knew it was not fair to these people to stay there with them, since they were not, as yet, suffering from this complaint. So just before we started I scrambled out and back to the crowded deck where the stretcher patients were lying, packed like sardines, and facing the glaring sun. Fortunately the rain had stopped. I saw a tiny ledge just below the tiny ship's bridge and out of everybody's way, so climbed up there and sent a message to Pat down below to join me. It was very hot there in the sun. The ledge was about four feet square, and Val Smith and Iole joined us.

Our sisters did a superb job getting all those sick people on board without an accident, and then they proceeded to nurse them.

As long as I live I will never forget Iole emptying and dragging bedpans in the sea. The Dutch nuns managed to get some bedpans with handles on board. We hadn't seen them before. Iole would tie a piece of rope through the handle, then she would get out on the six-inch ledge that ran round the *outside* of the ship. Pat and I would hold her hand and arm while she tossed the bedpan in the sea, and the drag every time nearly pulled her into the water. I can't remember how often the girl did that, but she must have done it fifty times. If ever anyone deserved a Victoria Cross she did.

During the afternoon a young Englishwoman died and was buried at sea. Extraordinarily enough, she had said some months before that she would like that to happen to her if she died in captivity. That burial was a nightmare.

That night we were very cold on our ledge. We took it in turns to sleep; only one could curl up on her side at a time. It wasn't too bad, since we had anchored just inside the entrance to the Musi River. We set off again up the river at dawn, the third trip in that same river, and arrived at Palembang well after midday. Twenty-six hours in that awful tub for those sick people, and everyone was sunburnt to glory.

As we pulled in—our ship was so small we were below the level of the wharf—we noticed some Japanese officers waiting there and looking down at us. We were quite pleased to see Yamasaki, one-time commandant of our camp for a month or so. We don't know why we were pleased to see him, but we were, not that any one of us liked him, but he had never worried us unduly.

He took one look at our deck, which was covered with dying women, and at the feeble efforts to protect them from the hot sun, and the smile went off his face very suddenly. He turned and spoke to another officer, who sent a third Jap running away for something. A few minutes later this person returned and gave something to the Jap we didn't know, who then jumped on to the deck and gave some injections to those desperately ill people. This is the first time we have seen a Jap actually do something to help the sick.

We had to get out on to the wharf and stand there for about an hour in twos for tenko while our nursing staff, the same six girls, once more carried the stretcher patients across the wharf, over dozens of railway tracks, and put them down on the grass. Jap orders. As soon as they got the last patient over there they were told to bring them all back to be counted! We were all counted, then once more the trek across the rails. It was a relief to sit on grass for an hour or so. We were then given something to drink, which came along in buckets carried by Jap underlings. It was hot and wet and we all enjoyed it.

At last a train came in, and we were told to get in. The stretcher patients were put into cattle trucks, the walking patients and others into carriages, filthy with black grit, but with padded seats, which rather surprised us. This was better than that blazing sun.

We had to sit there on a siding all night, with windows and doors closed, blinds down and no light. It was airless and pitch dark. We sat there and stifled and put in another hellish night sitting up. Six of the patients in the cattle trucks died that night before we ever left the siding. There is no doubt about it, everything is done that can be done to break up our morale and kill us off, but we are not cracking, Mr Jap!

As we had eaten sour, cold rice only on that journey, we were quite amazed when a Jap boarded the train during the night and called out, "*Roti!*"—which means "bread". We haven't seen bread since we were first interned, and it sounded too good to be true. It wasn't actually bread; nobody ever found out what it was, but it was good. It was hard and brown and very heavy. Each loaf was about four inches long and about two inches thick and must have weighed about a pound. Some said it was made of rubber because it was very chewy, but as one of these loaves each was our ration until we arrived in camp two days later we found it much better than rice, in spite of its toughness. We found it so hard to break a mouthful off. It did wonders for most people and seemed to stop diarrhoea at once.

At 7 a.m. we started and, once on the move, were allowed to raise the blinds and windows a little to get some fresh air. Each time we passed a station we had to pull the blinds down again so the locals could not see us. This was a silly idea, because it didn't stop a few pineapples and bananas being bought from natives *en route*. The Japs had also sold us some very expensive, very green bananas and a few green pine-apples, far too green to eat, so it made more for us to carry.

Val Smith was O.C. fruit and walked the length of the train many times trying to please everybody. Iole was busy organizing one carriage as a hospital; it had two long seats down the side and a long table down the centre. So many people were ill and more getting ill, and everybody was absolutely worn out. Iole arranged for every sick person to be able to lie down on these long seats and stretch out for a couple of hours at a time until all had a rest. A Jap doctor appeared during the day and Iole and Val said they must have quinine, since so many patients were down with malaria. He staggered the two girls by asking how much they needed and gave them the amount they asked for!

We passed some very interesting country going across Sumatra in this train. We saw the most peculiar-shaped mountains, very steep and abrupt looking, and some beautiful rivers, lush-looking green jungles, and thousands of tropical fruit-trees, most of them laden with fruit.

We eventually arrived at Loebok Linggau at 8 p.m. Most of us jumped off the train to get a breath of fresh air, but we were made to get back in again to spend the night once more in that thick atmosphere. For three nights running we all sat up; we were nearly dead with weariness, thirst and hunger, yet those two sisters of ours had to put up with these conditions and help the sick, who were getting worse, and others becoming ill all the time. Iole and Val didn't sit down for more than ten minutes at a time during the whole of the journey in that train.

At 5 a.m., just before dawn, we were all hurried out by screaming Japs with notice for all to get ready. We were just pushed out and, as they were swinging their bayonets in the region of our legs again, we were out pretty smartly.

The very sick people on stretchers were taken out of the cattle trucks and once more put on the wet grass, where all were given a hot drink, nobody knows what. Those women lying there in the half-light looked shocking. Dr McDowell looked like a limp rag; she had worked hard all night and all day in the cattle trucks with the sick. She was marvellous. Of course, more died during the journey, and we had many more people who would have to go straight into hospital on arrival.

About an hour or so later we were all bundled into trucks and driven at that Jap crazy speed through the freezing early morning air to a rubber plantation about twelve miles out from the town. We passed hundreds of laden banana palms, and the roadside was lined with tapioca plants. We arrived at the camp soon after 8 a.m. and were met by Woodie, Jennie Greer, Win Davis, Jess Doyle, and a few English nurses. It was good to see them. They thought we all looked awful and were very concerned about us, but what a relief to have that hell journey behind us!

The first thing I saw was a huge heap of sweet potatoes. What a change from sour, dry, cold rice! Win said they had been given sweet potato stew that had *carrot* in it, and she had kept a spoonful each for us. That is Win, always doing something for others. It was luscious.

The stretcher patients were carried up a slope, then down a muddy and treacherous incline to a creek, across a narrow, wet, and slippery bridge, past the community kitchen and across flat ground for about three hundred yards alongside the creek to the tiny hospital. We walking patients collected our gear and started off behind the others. What a thrill to have plenty of shade from hundreds of rubber-trees and to have running water in the creek for the camp!

This camp is in the middle of an unused rubber estate, which appears to have been wrecked by the Dutch before they left it and to have grown wild ever since. Most internees are living in large, badly built attap huts with leaking roofs and sides and mud floors. All sleep on bali bali. These huts are up on the hill on the far side of the creek from the hospital. On the flat side of the creek is the lower camp where the British and Dutch kitchen staff live beside the community kitchen. Farther on past this kitchen block is a one-roomed cottage with a balcony where eighteen Charitas nuns live in what is called Hut 12. Next door to them is a smaller one-roomed hut where ten Australian sisters live—in Hut 13! These nuns and nurses are the hospital staff, the hospital being about two hundred yards past these two huts. The remaining Australian sisters live up on the hill at the top of the camp. They are the district nurses and will look after all those living up there with them. There must be six hundred people living up there and they have to carry every drop of water they want from the creek.

Pat and I were discharged from hospital the day after we arrived, Pat going up to be a district nurse and I joining the hospital staff in Hut 13.

We are back on the sloping bali bali again, but this time we have boards and not branches to lie on. This is much more comfortable, but full of bugs and rats. We have about twenty-two inches of bed-space each. We seem to be packed in again, but we do have a concrete floor and galvanized-iron roof, so can keep dry. We are in the prettiest little gully, and the creek flows only ten yards away from the door, full of rocks and lined with ferns. Could almost believe we are up in the hills near Gembrook at home! If only we didn't have eight lavatories built over the creek and looking like tiny bathing boxes, right in front of our front door, it would be almost perfect.

All the first day I couldn't help singing "All Things

Bright and Beautiful" as we settled in to this tiny place, but it rained hard all night, and in the morning we were horrified to see the creek had risen and our hut was surrounded by water two feet deep. We were isolated. I was forced to change my tune to "River, Stay 'Way from my Door". However, it subsided in twenty-four hours and left us surrounded in mud.

There are not any bathrooms, the drill being to bathe in the stream in front of House 12, next door. The Japs have measured off a portion of the creek here by stringing attap across from one bank to the other, forming a "swimming pool" about fifty yards long. This does not protect us from the eyes of the hay-hoes and Jap guards, who lounge about under trees farther up the bank and watch us, blast them. They have quite an uninterrupted view, being only a dozen or so yards from the bathers.

All cooking water is drawn from the creek beside the kitchen, which of course is upstream a little way from the swimming pool and lavatories. We can't swim, since it is only a foot deep and very rocky, but we can have a good wash in running cool water.

We find we can eat most of the grass growing near the creek, also the young curling fronds of ferns. Curried fern with sweet potato is exactly like eating mushrooms!

Very soon after we arrived in this camp Miss Dryburgh died. That awful move from Muntok was too much for her. What a wonderful person she was, and how hard she worked to give the people in the camp such pleasure! With the help of Norah Chambers she wrote all the music for the "orchestra", the words and music of all the songs for the glee singers, anthems for the church choir, two books of poems, stories, etc. She was also co-editor of a camp magazine which was sent round to all internees twice a month in the early days—a magazine with interest for everybody, containing articles, camp news, crossword puzzles, competitions, recipes, and so on. Unfortunately the magazine only lasted a few months, owing to the lack of paper. Miss Dryburgh's death has caused much sadness throughout the whole camp.

8th May 1945. We have been here for nearly a month, and so far no sign of the Red Cross parcels promised us. They are here, up at the guard-house, but the Japs won't give them to us, because the Americans sank the ship that was carrying the receipt for them! What will they think up next?

A few days ago mail arrived, and what a day! Every one of us received a large bundle from home. Iole at last has heard from her family; we both received twenty letters, most of them containing twenty-five words only. They were all dated 1942 and 1943—only three years old! Some of us received our first snaps from home. I get my three out twice a day and gaze with increasing wonder at the fat on everybody, such fat legs on the children compared with the poor little children in camp here. Guess we must all look pretty skinny and have got used to seeing thin people around the place. Very few of us have a tail to sit on these days, mostly bone, and our legs look just like bones re-covered with some skin. I know I can grip my wrist and my upper arm and lap over with finger and thumb. Well under six stone now.

Starvation has set in again. We were so thrilled with the different vegetables here, carrots, chokos, bringals, decent long beans—certainly in small quantities, but definitely a change. Now they have all stopped and the diet is rice and sweet potatoes. The potatoes are brought to the guard-house just outside the barrier, dumped in the nearest pool of water, and left there in the sun and rain for three or four days. When they are thoroughly bad we may take them into the camp and eat them.

12th May 1945. My mistake, we are getting a few vegetables every three days now. The same drill about leaving them in the sun and rain for a couple of days before we can get at them. For lunch on the first day of receiving them we have carrot and turnip tops, on the second day we have their bottoms, and on the third day what is left, usually fern leaves, lily stalks etc. and of course a few over-ripe sweet potatoes. So far in this camp we have had meat, which looked like bullock, twice. A piece weighing about five pounds was brought in on each occasion to feed six hundred and forty people!

14th May 1945. My fourth birthday in this camp. Iole said that "fortunately" she had malaria yesterday, so couldn't eat her rice at tea-time. It was produced early this morning, fried up with sweet-potato leaves from the new garden we made alongside Hut 13, as a present. We both thoroughly enjoyed it. Val Smith produced a miniature model of Jap guard "Bully", complete with three red stars on his collar, which she made from a piece of old khaki shirt and stuffed with rag. Later in the day I was found to be carrying a small flea on me and the doctor told me I had a spot on my lung, so everything is fine!

We are finding it hard to cope with fleas and bugs, in spite of keeping our hut spotlessly clean. These things come up out of the cracks in the bali bali at night. Every morning we take everything we own out into the sun for a while for airing and have to de-bug our mosquito nets well and truly. We have so many dozens of joins and seams in these nets that bugs creep in and settle down so quickly that we are forced to do this revolting chore each morning.

We are all getting malaria every few days, temperatures range about the 104°-105° mark, but Blanchie is still immune. She is the only one of us who has not had malaria. She often laughs about it and says she is missing out on something. Most of us have beriberi as well. Chris Oxley and I go nearly mad with what we call our "red patches". They are red, hot, terribly painful patches which show up on our legs about once a week. They make us feel quite sick. The next day the redness disappears, but is replaced by stiffness in the muscles of our legs, so much so that we can hardly walk and certainly cannot bend our knees. The third day the stiffness has gone, but we are so swollen we look like fat pigs, the swelling and puffiness going farther up our bodies with each attack. Fourth day, everything normal once more and peace reigns in our bodies.

16th May 1945. We are all very amused today. These Japs have done mighty little for us other than starve us and keep our Red Cross parcels, and now they have announced that a Jap band, of all awful things, is coming to entertain us to-morrow. We suppose that is the last item on their list of "How to Treat Prisoners". This is to cheer us up, we suppose

26th May 1945. The Jap military band was a huge success! As it was on top of the rise at the far end of the camp from here not one of us went, but at 2.30 p.m. along came "Gold Teeth", the new interpreter, and he screamed at us to *"lekas"* ("hurry") up the hill. He was furious and was swinging a great stick wildly over our heads, so we did not waste any time and all scrambled up that steep bank to the top of the camp.

We were amazed at what we saw. There were about thirty Japs *all dressed alike* and *all shaved*, a sight we had never seen, and their expressions were entirely different. There was no sign of hatred on their faces at all. They were simply men who loved good music and played it well.

They played all German music, mostly overtures and waltzes we all knew. One fellow sang a Japanese marching song. It was obvious that he was Western-trained. He had a delightful voice, even the Japanese words sounding soft and clear, not a bit like the "clack clack" of words we are so used to hearing.

Both band and audience were in beautiful surroundings, we were all in the shade of many rubber-trees. We sat on the ground or on trunks of fallen trees; the band had proper chairs they brought with them, as we haven't any here. The setting was really beautiful for our first taste of musical in-struments for many years. Most of us wanted to howl when the music started; I know I had a terrible struggle for the first ten minutes. For two hours we all forgot we were prisoners.

Mary Cooper, a nursing sister serving with Q.A.I.M.N.S., who has been here with us since the fall of Singapore, and who has been very ill in hospital for months, was suddenly called upon about a month ago by two Jap officers and told to hurry up and get well because she could go home to

M

Ireland. Just like that! They left a couple of ampules of something to be injected to help her get well.

Mary felt very mixed about the whole thing. She was desperately ill and she wanted to go home, but not alone like that. Nobody blamed her! At the time she was far too ill to be moved. Now, apparently, the situation has altered and it is all off; nothing further has been done.

A Swedish nursing sister, who was matron of a leper station out from Palembang somewhere before she was brought here to join us in 1943, has also been promised her freedom and told she may go back to Sweden, travelling with Mary as far as Ireland. Big query, when? Sister Palm is very excited about it and really believes she will get away soon. Good luck to her.

A rather amusing thing happened to me a few days ago. During siesta I thought I would go and draw some water from a concrete well near here, to be ready for our small kitchen supply. A nun from next door let me borrow her precious large tin to draw the water in. I tied a piece of rope to the handle and went to work. To my horror, the rope broke and the tin floated about on top of the water. As there was a ledge about five feet from the top, I got in and was able to reach the tin and throw it out, but I couldn't get out myself. First thing I did was to get the giggles, which always come across me in an impossible situation. I called for help, but nobody heard, so I had to stay there until somebody walked by. When one of our girls came along I nearly frightened the life out of her by yelling from the well. Reinforcements came and helped me out. Never again! Next time I drop a tin in the well it will have to stay there if I can't poke it out.

Chickens and ducks have started to come in for hospital patients. A call for volunteers to undress them was answered. Finally I found myself on the chicken- and duck-plucking staff for hospital. The poor birds are so thin they look as if they probably welcomed death. The patients have to pay the Japs forty-five guilders for each bird.

I am an assistant to Miss Hartley, who tells me she has lived life in the raw with her family in Malayan jungles. They all worked for the Malayan Government in some forestry job. She has many interesting tales of their jungle life, how they killed and skinned wild animals, including tigers. I am fascinated by the way she strips the birds while I hold this part and that part after we have plucked them. The wings and legs are removed first, then the shoulders and back, and I am left holding a neat little chassis, with all the insides looking at me, which are then removed by one movement of her hand. No mess at all, and the bird is in pieces and ready for the cook.

My remuneration for services rendered is one head and a handful of intestines, which I take home and clean in the creek, then make the most tasty chicken broth! The only bits we can't eat are the eyes and the beak. Chicken's eyebrows are a delicacy, and as for the brain—! It is a bit small, but very sweet.

We ten are all working very hard at the hospital, which is packed with patients the whole time. We can't last long at a time on duty now, an hour being as much as anyone can take. After a break we can do another hour. Any tropical ulcers or infected cuts or bites, are treated by pouring on red palm-oil, which is kept in a beer bottle, then by covering with bits and pieces of old rag. Our friend the nun in Hut 12 still boils up the oil-drum each morning, so she boils these little pieces of rag for us and they dry quickly in the strong sunlight. This is the best we can do. Quite a lot of time is spent making patients eat; we sit there for hours beside them on the bali bali feeding them half a teaspoonful every five minutes. We have discovered that no matter how ill a person is she can't afford to miss her rice. If they absolutely refuse and make it impossible for us they soon die. It is very grim nursing.

27th May 1945. We are tasting life in the raw now, and how! In Muntok we had thin, very thin, wild goat, and had two soft turtle eggs. Last week we had one tiny monkey brought in to make a stew for over six hundred people. It was horrible. Hungry as we are, we won't eat monkey again. It smelt to high heaven.

Last night we celebrated some excellent news we heard. Nobody knows the source of the story, but we were told that the war with Germany is finished. Thank goodness for that! Those wonderfully brave people in England will have some peace at last. We thought the war in Europe finished just before last Christmas, but we must have been a bit previous. We have also been told that the Americans have taken a small island beginning with O to the south of Japan, and taken it at a terrific cost. This should give them a good base for attacking Japan direct. That is what we have been wanting to hear for ages.

If this is all true, it should not be long now before these little yellow devils are finished off. How they hate us!

31st May 1945. Another one of our sisters died today, Gladys Hughes, the only New Zealander amongst our group of Army nurses. This is getting worse and worse.

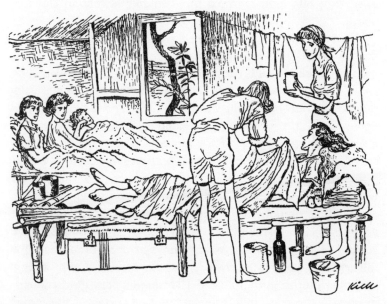

Chapter 23

10th June 1945. We are still eating peculiar things. We had deer one day about a week ago, a huge old animal, and it was excellent. A few days later we had what we thought was tiger meat, bad and very high. It was eaten because the smell left it after it was cooked. So far, no ill effects. The carrots didn't last long and we are back to the old diet of tapioca leaves and that bitter jack fruit. Rations are still left outside in the weather for a couple of days before we get them, but we are getting used to it now.

The creek has flooded again and down the stream came logs of wood, fallen trees, and other debris. As we are desperate for wood Blanchie, Flo Trotter, and I went in after a tree. We dragged it on to the bank, then got back into the stream and had a grand old swim! The water was deep and cold and it was most stimulating being rushed down with the tide. We did not allow ourselves to go far because of the rocks, now hidden. We were blue with cold when we came out, but soon warmed up—couldn't help it in this hot place.

We need and use such a lot of wood here. All rice for the day is cooked by ten o'clock in the morning in the community kitchen, and then handed out to the blocks. The cooks are not strong enough to do more than this. We always reheat the rice by frying it for midday and evening meals behind our little hut in what we call our kitchen. The fireplace is made from two pieces of train line we found, which are balanced on bricks. Quite effective, too, if we have enough wood.

There are plenty of dead rubber-trees outside the barbed wire, but we are not allowed to get them, so when the crack of a falling branch inside the camp area is heard everyone drops everything and dashes off to recover the wood. We are getting quite good at throwing things at dead branches until the precious wood falls down. Throwing a piece of rope over a branch is another idea. Iole and Val found a very dead rubber-tree across the creek in a far-away, unused corner of the camp. They worried and pushed that tree until it fell down with an almighty crash. They looked like a couple of terriers annoying a draught-horse. The hospital patients watching them were in fits of laughter. The tree then had to be broken up and carried home.

The cemetery is just outside the camp on a hill about three hundred yards up from the hospital. It is quite a pretty spot amongst trees, ferns, and wildflowers. Many people go to funerals just to get firewood. Most of them come back into camp dragging dead branches of trees behind them. It does seem so awful to be forced to do this, but it is the only way to get enough wood to cook meals.

More of our sisters are in hospital now, all of them very ill. If we don't get out of here within the next few months many more of our girls won't make it. Food is coming into the camp, but not for us who do all the nursing without a let-up. It is for the "hard workers". But every now and then we can buy a little from a Chinese who calls sometimes.

We were all invited to a dance and pork supper by the

Japanese a few days ago! Dance? Why, we can hardly walk! A few of the Japs' "girl-friends", who are Eurasians in camp with us, went along and danced. Next day we had what was left of the pork. The Japanese order was to divide it between hospital patients and hospital staff. It was jolly good, too. We had one pig's trotter between us as our share, and sucked the bones all dry.

Workers belong to squads who go out of camp and chop down rubber-trees. We did it for a while, but could not last too long and had no energy at all. The first working squads in this camp had to go for quite a long walk to a main road, then they had to remove a great heap of stones from the side of the road and put them in a heap on the other side about twenty yards farther down. Next time they went out they had to put the same stones back in their original position! We had more to do with our time than that, so now the workers are nearly all Indo-Dutch, Indonesians, Eurasians, and some of the big boys. They get sugar, bananas, extra rice, and an extra ration of vegetable in return for services rendered. Lately they have been working near the camp felling rubber-trees and dragging them into camp for the community kitchen fires. It looks as if it is more sabotage than wood for our kitchen fires.

We Australians have done more than our fair share of chopping trees, digging drains, and clearing roadways for the last three years and simply haven't time or strength to go out on these squads now. We are all working ourselves to a standstill nursing and doing our own chores in order to make life bearable.

One day last week a Dutch patient with very little wrong with her was terribly rude to one of our girls and wanted more attention than she was getting. The girl looking after her should have been a patient herself, for she was not properly over an attack of malaria. She suddenly got wild and said, "Anyone would think you were paying us four guineas a week." The answer came, "What is guinea?" and our friend just burst out laughing. "Forget it!" she said.

Tenko still goes on at 7 a.m. and 5 p.m. daily. We now have to stand outside the hut next door and be there, even if the guard has not arrived, a few minutes before that time. We don't like Amana, he is a sneaking type of fellow. He sometimes takes a short cut through the rubber and lands on us from a different angle and gets furious when someone is missing. The missing member is always watching the fire so that the hut won't burn down.

Kong can get away with being late every time. She calmly strolls over when *she* is ready, and all guards wait for her and say nothing. Japs don't know what to do with the Chinese; they are certainly too scared to punish them.

One day in hospital the glass funnel of an oil-lamp was broken. The Jap in charge of the camp was jumping mad and said to send the culprit to the guard-house to stand there at attention all day. Kong wandered up to the guard-house, said the wind had broken the lamp, and walked away again. A new glass funnel arrived later in the day!

We are getting red palm-oil again, and in large quantities. It looks exactly like thick tomato soup. We have missed it very much in the last six months. The only red palm-oil we had was the small amount used for dressings in the hospital. Now we use it for lighting in the huts. Instead of going to bed in the dark we put some oil in a small tin, place a piece of wire or strip of tin across the top, then drag a piece of rag as a wick through the wire. The light is good enough to help us see our way to bed and put up our mosquito nets.

We now have enough oil for all our cooking and, as it is said to be full of vitamins, this should help us. Some of the planters' wives with us said it was used in Malaya before the war by the natives and their families working on the rubber estates.

17th June 1945. What are we coming to? Life here is certainly interesting. Two Indonesian families, each with half a dozen children, have taken to eating snakes, and as this camp is full of them they are not hard to obtain. We also heard that they are eating rats, since they must have their protein.

Maybe they are right, maybe they are wrong, but one member of the snake- and rat-eating family was taken to hospital very suddenly in a most peculiar condition and died a few hours later.

We have been told these families will pay two guilders and fifty cents for a rat, so yesterday we tried them out. A small rat was discovered swinging in Blanchie's corn basket, which was hanging from the roof on a piece of wire. Blanchie jumped up out of bed—it was very early in the morning—and called out, "Hooray, I've got two-fifty in my basket!" She dressed herself quickly and went off with it to the Indos in Hut 11. Unfortunately the rat got out of the basket just as she was delivering it, so Blanchie went without her money. However, the price was wrong, she was offered only one guilder twenty cents. Perhaps it was on the small side.

18th June 1945. Today shop came in and we were able to buy one handful of baby onions, one handful of peanuts in their shells, and one small egg, no bigger than a bantam's egg. The total cost of these things in Australian money would be twenty-one shillings!

Three tiny eggs came for ten people, so we produced a pack of cards to draw and see which end of the hut should start on eggs. We had been told they would come to us three at a time until everybody had one. Vivian was at one end of the hut, I was at the other, and while everybody involved kept fingers crossed we drew our cards. I drew first—the three of spades. My friends did glare at me! Vivian then drew a three of diamonds! Of course we all roared with laughter and people came from all over the place to see what the noise was all about. Only an egg!

There are three planters' homes on top of the hill outside the camp, about a quarter of a mile away, which have recently been occupied by German women and children. They are well dressed and appear to be well fed and look like the normal people we used to see in pre-war days. Where they have come from we do not know, but we have been told to share our food with them.

Our people have to go and collect their food buckets at meal-times, carry them that long distance down the hill and over the slippery old bridge to the kitchen for their rations, then carry them back up hill again.

There is strictly no communication allowed between the two camps; we must not address them at all, and a Jap guard always accompanies the food-carriers to see that this rule is carried out.

One of the Germans from this community is in our hospital now with dystentery, and the Japs are in a flap trying to get something to cure her. I might add she isn't nearly as ill as our own people. She is nursed in a corner of the ward with a Jap guard near by all the time to make sure we don't ask questions. She is a very pleasant person, speaks good English, and is most upset about our condition and conditions. Her ten stone looks very solid against our light weights. This German woman gave Iole a pair of silk stockings for nursing her. Iole doesn't know what to do with them, but perhaps they can be sold for food later on.

26th June 1945. No Ireland for poor little Mary Cooper. She couldn't make the grade and died this morning. Mary was an awfully nice girl, only in her twenties, too.

Sister Palm has gone on her first lap to Sweden. She left the camp in Siki's beautiful sedan. We hear she is in Palembang only, and staying with a Swiss family there. We think that will be as near to Sweden as she will get before the end of the war.

6th July 1945. Rat- and snake-eating has been prohibited by the doctors!

Things are certainly grim, but somehow there is always something to laugh about. On duty at the hospital today, I was asked, in Dutch, to give a "clisma" to another woman from the German community outside the camp who was in our hospital. After scratching about looking for bits and pieces to do this, I eventually went into action. It was quite an international event—an Australian nurse, instructed by a Dutch nun, to give treatment to a German woman in the presence of a Japanese soldier! First thing I did was to put the Jap outside the door; he seemed quite willing to go when he saw all the apparatus ready. The patient told me they were all very upset about us and would like to help us, but the guards watch them too closely for them to be able to do anything effective.

8th July 1945. More cables and letters have come for us from home. They are 1943 and early 1944 ones this time. Japs must have been hoarding them for some time. Thank goodness our people put the year on their letters! We can work out how old new nephews and nieces are by now. My two cables told me of the death of my brother two years ago, which broke me completely. Another snap arrived, it just popped out of an envelope and showed my sister's family. Anthony, a little boy of three when I left home, now a lanky schoolboy, and a little girl of about two sitting there, quite a stranger to me, but somehow familiar. What fun meeting these children when I go home!

The news from Australia has us quite baffled. Most of our brothers and cousins are being demobbed. Is the war over? Letters from England and Scotland talk of people getting back to pre-war jobs and others going on holidays. One woman in camp told us her husband was back in Bangkok opening a bank there. A British army engineer, brother to one of the English sisters here with us, is out of the army and is helping with the reconstruction of bridges in Burma!

The only war gossip we have heard lately is that the Japs are going to get us all out of Sumatra and give the country its independence, as they say they have done in other countries they have taken. We should hate to see this rich country run by the types we have seen loose in it.

19th July 1945. Win Davis, our "Winnie May", died today, after being desperately ill for some weeks, poor kid. It was her thirtieth birthday only a week or so ago. Somehow I can't imagine not seeing Win again—to die now after all these awfully long years of internment. . . . I shall never forget how wonderful Win was to me during my first weeks of internment when my fingers were burnt and bandaged, and for so long I was so useless. Win always helped me out. Pat Gunther worked wonders getting eggs and English potatoes on the black market, which is very difficult here, to save Win from eating rice. They were great friends. We all did everything we could, but we couldn't save her.

We are having trouble with the wild animals wandering through this uncared-for rubber estate, which is now overgrown jungle in some places. Every night some heavy animal comes down the slope on the opposite bank of the creek and jumps into the water, where it makes very peculiar noises, almost as if it were straining food through its snout. There is a lot of mushy stuff that floats down from the kitchen, rotting vegetables and left-overs that can't be cooked. This is the only way to get rubbish out of the camp, and we have to dodge it all the time we are washing ourselves or our belongings. That is why we don't feel clean now after we have washed.

Val Smith is sure this animal is a wild boar, and some bright soul suggested Val should catch it and kill it, the idea being to grab it by its tail, if it has one!

The other night I could not get to sleep. It was hot and airless, and as I seemed to be disturbing the others I went outside and walked along the track towards the hospital. It was a glorious moonlight night, far too good to waste in internment, and I stood for a while gazing at the beauty of the moonlight through the trees and on the ferns and rocks. Suddenly I heard a gentle, quiet pit-pat ahead, and there, coming along the path towards me, was a very pretty deer with two tiny ones trotting gently beside it. It looked like a Christmas card. I kept quite still, but they saw me, jumped into the creek, and hurried away out of sight.

This was quite a different experience to others in the camp. One night a guard went flying past us, minus his rifle, at terrific speed, and we wondered why. He had been guarding the hospital. One of the doctors started out from her hut to go to the hospital at the same time as the guard ran, but she dashed back inside, too. There was a tiger just a few yards away! It apparently did not like the look of the place because it wandered away again, but reappeared in the camp on top of the hill on two or three occasions. So far nobody is missing.

We are still having peculiar things to eat, but we are gradually getting a little protein in our diet, even if it is only a teaspoonful of meat. Today we had bear to eat, and after the kitchen staff had it cleaned and ready to cook along came some Jap guards and removed all the fat *and* the two hind legs.

20th July 1945. Must mark this date to check up on what has happened in the world outside. On those rare occasions when we get pork it is usually part of a wild pig for the whole camp. Today we were given fourteen live pigs to be killed, cut up, rationed out, and given uncooked to the people. All the insides, plus noses, ears, and tails are going to be made into one huge stew in the community kitchen. Because we ten helped in the big kill we were given a loin part, which contained nine chops. This made it very awkward, but we got over it. Iole and I were the hut cooks that day, so we pot roasted it. We made an onion gravy and it was absolutely delicious. It was the largest piece of meat we had had for years, so kept our piece of chop bone to have another chew later in the day. None of us realized how much flavour there is in a bone. We all feel very comfortable inside.

21st July 1945. We had a super stew today, almost a cupful. It contained the etceteras of the pigs, and was so rich we could not eat it all in one sitting. Most of us kept half to have with our rice at tea-time. We feel so full of energy now that we have something solid inside.

An old dead rubber-tree was felled in front of our hut yesterday. Most of it went into the creek and started to float away. People in the hut across the river started gathering the wood on the bank, so two of our girls went into the creek after the trunk. They needed help, so away eight of us went and waded down the rocky bed of the stream towards Val, who, in spite of an attack of malaria she was having, was holding on to this big thing for all she was worth. By this time it was in quite a deep part of the creek. It was an awful job stumbling round the creek trying to get that trunk out of the water and, as usual, we all got the giggles and were helpless. However, we finally got it out and now have enough firewood to last us for months. Jess had bad luck and cut her feet quite badly on the rocks.

26th July 1945. A little more mail from home. Iole is terribly worried about her young brother in the R.A.A.F. All her 1943 letters say he is "missing over Germany". We are in a maddening situation here.

Another thing that worries us is that we are running out of coconut fibre. We use it for toothbrushes, with ash from the fireplace for tooth-paste. Our mouths never feel clean now.

Jess is in hospital. Her feet are badly infected and look awful. No more wading in stony creeks for her for a while.

August 1945. Dorothy Freeman, who was my senior in pre-war training days in Melbourne and worked for so long in the bakery business with Iole, Rene, and me, having lots of fun with us, died on 8th August. For some time she had been getting a lot of malaria, dysentery, and beriberi, which would not let up. She was in hospital and died quite suddenly one night just after she and Flo Trotter had had a cup of tea and a chat. Flo was on night duty and was terribly shaken, as we all were.

We must get out of here soon, or we shall lose more of our girls. Mitz is very sick now and in hospital, and we are all about at the end of our tether. Pat Black, Jennie Greer, and Woodie are ill, too, not in hospital, but being nursed by our sisters in the huts on the hill. Tweedie looks terrible, but still persists in doing too much. She has lost almost seven stone so far. God, what guts these girls have! They are a grand lot.

Shortie looks as if she would blow over if she went outside into the wind. Our little hut of ten always has three or four down at the same time with malaria or something else, and it is getting increasingly difficult to go on nursing in the hospital. Quite often Jean Ashton and Wilma Oram do double hospital duty in one day because somebody has suddenly been stricken in our hut. These two girls must be made of cast iron. Jean has worked like a slave ever since she was taken prisoner.

17th August 1945. Wilma had her fourth birthday as a prisoner today. She is in her twenties, wasting the best years of her life. We had an afternoon-tea party, inviting our whole family and a few others along. Each person had to bring her own drinking bowl for coffee and her own sugar if she wanted any. Parties really are not much trouble here. About twenty-five of us had a tiny morsel of birthday cake, made from browned ground rice and cooked in a one-pound butter tin. It looked very forlorn sitting on an enamel plate while all these hungry women sat round waiting for some. Perhaps after we have all had four birthdays here we shall be able to have real cake for our celebrations.

Iole and I have quite good cooking utensils now. We boil our water and cook our vegetables in an old salmon tin with a tiny wire handle. This is our billy. Our frying pan is made from the lid of a Klim tin with a piece of barbed wire round it and twisted to form a handle. The barbs have been hammered with a stone to grip the rim of the lid, and the handle part has also been hammered until it is flat. Our stew pot is a tiny aluminium latex cup which we found amongst the rubber-trees. It is two inches deep and about two inches wide, also with a piece of wire round it to form a handle and hammered to make it grip the latex cup. This is big enough to heat up our stew rations, when we get stew, or to heat up other things.

There is always something to laugh at and talk about, but we are really very tired of this life here. We are now eating fried pumpkin flowers, dahlia leaves, and such stuff. Tapioca roots have been up on the hill lying in the sun and rain outside the camp entrance for days, but we are not allowed to have them yet. Perhaps the idea is the same as they had once before when we were in the men's camp last year. Then the tapioca roots were left in a heap outside our gate until they dissolved away. What peculiar mentalities these Japs have!

18th August 1945. Our dear Mitz died this afternoon, having been through a most uncomfortable few days. If only we could do something to help these sick girls! We never leave their sides and do all we can to make them comfortable. It is terrible to keep a sick girl warm by covering her with an old rice sack. These damned Japs won't give us a thing in the way of medical supplies; we all feel sure they have the stuff, but are just being thoroughly nasty about it, and won't give it to us. A year ago we saw them unpacking boxes of medical supplies sent by the American Red Cross, but we have never been given any of this.

Mitz, Sister Mittelheuser, was third senior sister in our hospital unit, 2/10th A.G.H., and had worked terribly hard in Malaya and Singapore. Then later in camp she worked like the Trojan she was as our house captain and housekeeper.

Of the sixty-five sisters who left Singapore we are now only twenty-four.

Pat, Iole, and Jess are now in hospital, and thank goodness they are getting better.

20th August 1945. We were very suddenly inspected yesterday by a high Japanese official. We were told to hurry up the hill and bring in the bad tapioca roots and distribute them throughout the camp before he arrived.

We then had to stand at attention beside our bed-space, not having time to get outside, and we had to bow to the brute and say our piece, which we all always have to do at tenko twice a day. We have to say, "*Hatti hatti homat.*" He was quite interested with what Siki called his "Australie kankafoos". He was a surly, sad-looking fellow with lots of gold braid on his coat and a huge patch on the seat of his pants.

Last Sunday the powers that be in the guard-house up the hill sent word round the camp that all the children could visit their fathers and brothers in the men's camp a mile or so away through the rubber. Flo and I were flat out cutting children's hair so they would look presentable. Never have we seen such frocking in all our camp lives. I shall never forget the sight of Leo as long as I live. Leo used to live with his family in our house back in 1943. He is now about six years old, quite black, with a squint and a missing front tooth. He was always naked. This day he was dressed in long brightly coloured pants made from a sarong, so long he kept walking on them. A very peculiar arrangement covered his chest and his hat looked as if it might have once been worn to a garden party by a film star! Leo was thrilled and came hurrying down to our hut to show us before he went off.

The little girls were sweet, dressed in frocks made at the last moment from some cast-offs, and each one wore a hair ribbon.

The excitement was at fever pitch when the bell rang for them to assemble at the guard-house. When they got there their names were listed and then their excitement died suddenly. The Japs called the names of those children who could not go, and that is how many wives and children learnt that their husbands and daddies had died, some of them more than a year ago. These beasts guarding us are a pack of sadists.

The children whose relatives were still alive visited the men and had a wonderful day. Some of the four-year-olds saw their daddies for the first time they would remember.

They came home full of chat and laden with parcels, notes, sweets, and bananas. All were impressed with the men's beards. "*My* daddy has hair all over his head and all over his face, too," said one five-year-old proudly. Some of them were frightened of the big men and cried until they came home. All were surprised to find such big men after seeing squat little Nipponese for so long.

One two-year-old was not allowed to go at all because he was too small to walk the distance. The guard told him he could go next year when he was bigger.

21st August 1945. Rumours, rumours, rumours. They all say the same thing. War is almost over and we are about to have peace. Other rumours say we are going to Australia, the English to Singapore, and the Dutch to Java. I couldn't count the number of times I have heard that one in the last three years! One thing is very noticeable, the guards seem to have their tails down and are not nearly as annoying as they were a few months ago.

Chapter 24

24th August 1945!

The war is over. Who will be first here to take us home? *We are free women!!!*[1]

26th August 1945. I was having a grand attack of malaria the day we heard, and couldn't write the wonderful news in my diary, but what happened was this:

A message was sent round the camp saying that Siki would be making one of his speeches up on the hill at 3 p.m. The rumours were getting stronger every hour and the excitement in the Indonesian block was terrific. They were certain the war was over. We all hoped Siki would tell us our rumours were true, but deep down inside we thought it would be his usual rubbish. After all, the end of the war would be a tremendous event, and why should it happen this day?

Some people said the war must be over, because the Chinese

[1] The war ended on 15th August 1945, but prison camps were not informed of this.

who brought in the rations said *"tabi mem"*, which is "good morning", for the first time in years. We were usually termed "orangs", which are pretty low types in any language.

Nobody could be bothered going up the hill to hear Siki, but after a while Blanchie and Flo Trotter wandered up just to put in an appearance. The rest of us went on with our chores or our malaria.

After a while Katrine, a Chinese girl who lives with the nuns next door, ran past and said to Sister James and myself, "War is finished at six o'clock tonight and big gate opened!" and ran on. We still thought it a rumour and didn't bother to tell the other girls, but we both had an odd, excited feeling inside us which refused to settle down. In a little while somebody else ran past and said the same thing, then Blanchie and Flo arrived back positively beaming and breathless, and said it was true. . . . Oh, what a glorious feeling!

Siki made a very short speech. He merely said, "War is ended, Americano and English will be here in a few days. We are now all friends!" He did not say who won the war.

Somebody made a huge tin of black coffee, and we celebrated and talked, but nobody was unduly excited, we were too stunned.

When we realized there wasn't any more of that awful tenko and standing outside bowing to these little horrors, no more face-slapping, no more standing in the sun for punishment, we started to get really excited, and by 6 p.m. the noise in the camp was terrific.

It is marvellous to be *free* and to be able to wander outside the barbed wire for a walk through the rubber and to collect some wood. How many thousands of times we have talked about being free, and now it is here everything seems just the same—*except* that the day after the announcement in came some vegetables for us, and boxes and boxes of medical stores, bandages, quinine, vitamin tablets, serums, powdered milk, butter, etc. All this stuff was carried down from the guard-house to the hospital.

There were dozens of enamel wash-basins, towels by the

score, and huge mosquito nets, almost young houses, made from cotton material that we at once tore into strips to make sheets and night attire. We shall be quite well stocked and living in comfort in a few days' time when the Allies come. All this must be the contents of the Red Cross parcels promised us early this year.

Shortie and I were allowed one day of freedom, then we were both put very smartly into hospital, fuming at the thought of missing the fun and games now going on. As we were admitted Jess and Iole were discharged so we could have their bed-space. We were told by the doctors it was to give us a rest before we started on our journey home. That sounded good enough for us, so in we went.

The thought that home is really in sight at last is almost too much to grasp. Home, the place we have had on our minds for the last few years till we have gone nearly crazy, is now a certainty this year. All of us can say now that we shall be home by next Christmas and know we are right this time. Last May I was chatting with one of the Indonesian women as we were doing our washing in the creek, and she told me then that we would be in Australia in September this year. Oh, I do hope it is true and we are all taken out of this death-trap quickly!

How lucky is a Dutch woman in hospital here! She was brought in early today suffering an agonizing pain. Her trouble was diagnosed as a ruptured gall bladder; the four women doctors immediately got in touch with a Japanese doctor and demanded instruments, anaesthetic, and other medical supplies and a place to operate.

A Dutch doctor was brought to a house up on the hill in the German settlement there. A room was prepared and an operation performed successfully. If this had happened a few days ago nothing could have been done—Japs never would co-operate. Two of our girls set up the operating theatre and assisted with the operation.

Amana, the guard, had the nerve to come round and call us to tenko yesterday morning. He got a very poor reception; we did not expect it and were not standing in two lines for him. He was furious and screamed at us, but we took no notice of him. Later Mrs Hinch reported him and he was punished in front of us by his superior officer. This freedom is going to be good!

Chris Oxley's luck is outstanding. For months now she has threatened to sell her four back teeth on their little gold bridge so she could buy food. As she was quite penniless she gave them to an Indonesian guard a few nights ago to sell for her on the black market. Next day we were told we were free. Poor Chris! We couldn't help laughing at her luck, and she laughed, too, but today the guard returned them to her. We were all quite surprised, because she said she didn't know which guard she gave them to and had really said good-bye to them.

27th August 1945. Most of us have been numb for the first few days of this freedom, but what really brought it home to us was when the civilian men from their camp a mile or two away on the same rubber estate walked into our camp to see their wives and families and took absolutely no notice of Siki. How we enjoyed seeing that! They walked straight past the Jap guards and did not even look their way.

There were very few British men left alive, but we were just as excited as anybody else to see real men at last and dressed in white shirts and shorts, after seeing nothing but bandy-legged monkeys dressed in khaki running around for three and a half years (and two weeks). These huge six-footers from Holland and a few of our own men have come here for the last three days and taken complete control of the camp. They have formed into working squads, chopping down trees near the kitchen to save carrying wood longer distances, into kitchen squads, food scouts, and so on. Last week our vegetable ration sat in the sun and rain for days, the best of it was picked out and fed to the pigs, the remainder to us. This week we have so much rice we can't cope with it all! The scouts have found a good supply of carrots. The kitchen today is full of rice and carrots.

We have had meat each day for three days now. Some of the men go out in the jungle and shoot wild pigs or deer, and they promise to keep up the supply. Instead of our usual little ration of gristle and skin we now have thick pork stew and plenty of it. As Shortie and I were in hospital we were given liver soup made specially for the patients. It was superb.

The men have also found lots of papayas, which are given to everybody in camp. This fresh fruit is going to work wonders for us all. They tell us the fruit is rotting on the trees outside the camp, and to think these nasty little Nips wouldn't let us have any! We should all be well again in no time.

One thing I forgot to mention—the very first thing the Japs gave us all, the day after Siki's speech, was a lipstick! One between two people. About an hour after that we were given a bottle of scent and a bottle of Chinese hair oil, also to be shared. It was most amusing to see women dashing about with crimson lips. It seemed to make their eyes shine, and we all looked so well! The scent is a bit overpowering, so we are not very interested in it.

Today "Dutchy" arrived on the door step of Hut 13. We have not seen Dutchy since February 1942. He was taken prisoner when we were at Muntok, and he helped us there quite a lot by "acquiring" food for us when we were so terribly hungry during those first two awful weeks. The girls said he arrived laden with food and announced that he had come to cook all day for the whole group of Australian nurses. At the moment I have only half finished a huge lunch he sent over here. The rest will have to wait until later on in the afternoon. It is fried rice and chicken, wonderful.

Yesterday the men brought more goods which they had found somewhere, and we were given half a bar of Jap soap, awful stuff, and one small cake of our own decent civilized soap, three packets of Japanese cigarettes, also a four-ounce tin of Australian butter. Shortie and I are to share the butter, but as we have had so much good, rich pork in the last few days, we thought if we opened the butter that would probably finish us off. After all we have not had any butter for three and a half years.

Today we were able to buy a "koekje", a small sweet biscuit, so we opened the tin of butter and put some on our cake. It was good! We also had a teaspoonful of bacon given to us, which we ate as soon as we got it.

All I want now is home and mother, a bottle of icy-cold lemonade, and some bread and jam. It is almost too much to believe that this may all happen any day.

Still 27th August 1945. I have written this diary spasmodically for three and a half years, but now it is written almost hourly because good things are happening so quickly. Hell has turned into heaven almost overnight. Thank goodness this diary does not have to be hidden any more, it looks a wreck.

The men are here in hoards to mend our leaking roofs, cutting firewood a decent size, making bridges at the hospital doorways to save us walking and falling in thick mud and water, and doing the cooking. They even send round a menu! This is in Dutch, of course, but that is easy to read when you are longing for a change in the diet.

Now at 4 p.m. comes the message: "No more money troubles, the Dutch Government will send in food and will pay for it." What a relief that is, after living on our wits, more or less, all this time, trying to earn money to buy miserable bits of food to keep body and soul together!

28th August 1945. The men have organized us properly and their kitchen staff is doing a wonderful job. They cook and serve food properly and it is still hot when we get it. Our kitchen staff had been too tired to be able to do it properly, and there were few people well enough to help them. They must have shouted for joy when the men arrived to take over.

Today our lunch rice was fried in pork fat and had little pieces of pork through it; yesterday we had curried pork with our rice. Apparently the shooting efforts of the men in the jungle are most successful. Thank you, men. Fowls and eggs are now beginning to appear on the scene.

I have never thought much about the hair on men's legs before, but at the moment a large Dutchman is working just outside the hospital doorway, making a decent path, and his hairy legs are a delight to gaze upon after seeing shiny, hairless, bandy yellow legs for so long.

Stop Press. Sister Palm is said to be at Benkoelen, about one hundred miles away, not in Sweden.

29th August 1945. Did some bartering with a native today, so the Malay we have been learning really works. He gave me fifteen bananas for a few Jap cigarettes. Tomorrow he said he will bring me ten eggs for ten cigarettes. We shall all be able to have an egg.

The natives wander through the camp now with fowls and bananas. They want clothes. They must be hard up if they want our clothes, which were old when we got them. They also want cigarettes.

Today we all had half a cup of milk, the first for years. We are getting bacon and papaya each day. It is a wonderful feeling not to be ravenously hungry all day long. This is fun being a patient, quite a change from nursing.

31st August 1945. It is Queen Wilhelmina's and Pat Gunther's birthday today and we have had an absolute feast day. The natives gave us a huge bullock and the men skinned and cooked it. We had our first taste of real beef for three years and plenty of it, too. It was as good as any I have had. It is such a novelty to be able to bite on something and chew it after rice, rice, rice. This meat each day is working wonders on us all. We have also had more butter given to us, and we are definitely beginning to feel more human and less like drooping lilies.

3rd September 1945. Out of hospital again, thank goodness. When I was discharged I walked over to Hut 13 and found all the girls sitting there chatting to Australian and Dutch men, the girls looking quite dashing with their lipstick. As I walked in all the men stood up. It quite startled me, it was so unlike life in the camp to see civilized manners again.

o

Things are coming in each day now. They have apparently been here for ages—things we have asked for over and over again, medicines we begged for and were refused, so our women died. To think they had so much stuff so close to our camp—blankets, mattresses, more boxes of medicines, materials for dresses, undies, silk stockings—and more hair oil! Butter is coming in each day; we were given a pound tin each today, so we are all letting our heads go and having it with every meal. We were also given a good ration of Jap tinned meat, it is quite good.

7th September 1945. Today we have all been issued with Japanese military shirts, shorts, hobnailed boots, and their army-issue black rubber boots, which we call sneakers. We look like a lot of tough guys, but it is a grand feeling to have something on our feet at last. The girls say the leather boots are comfortable, though very heavy, and are a great help getting through the mud. Shockingly coloured cotton materials are coming in, so we shall soon have a wardrobe.

3 p.m. The Allies have arrived! ! !

Two very young Dutch soldiers and a Chinese military man arrived today as advance guard to the Army of Occupation. They had been dropped by parachute a few days ago and were most impressed with our camp apparently, their first English words being, "What a bloody mess!"

They said they had never seen such awful conditions, and were amazed that anyone could live like this. It is not easy. Those men will be staying at Loebok Linngau, twelve miles away, and with their radio will report to their Headquarters in Colombo.

We are very interested to learn that Admiral Lord Louis Mountbatten is Supreme Allied Commander in this theatre of war, and is in Colombo. Of course, we don't know anything yet.

9th September 1945. The Dutchmen made the Japs take them to all their local storehouses and one was found to be packed to the ceiling with large five-pound tins of Australian butter, which was transferred in trucks to our camp store-house, a place never used by us as we had nothing to store. I was helping our rations people to divide the tins into so many per block. when over in a corner of the storehouse I saw a piece of newspaper sticking out. The thought went through my mind, "If that is not a piece of Melbourne *Herald* I'll go he!" I pulled it out, and there it was, the *Herald*, Thursday evening, with a date in August 1943. It was the page advertising the programmes of suburban picture shows, including the one nearest to my home. I took this piece of newspaper back to our hut and found it to be most popular with the Victorians. We sat down and read every word.

Our Dutch paratroops came into camp again today and had quite a long chat with us in our hut. They have great hopes of getting us all out of here fairly soon. What game men! They had a revolver each and that is all to protect themselves.

11th September 1945. Cheers and more cheers. We have been discovered by two young Australian paratroops who visited our camp today and came straight past everybody until they landed on the doorstep of our Hut 13. Viv, who is usually unmoved and very quiet, came rushing in, face positively crimson, and panted, "Australians are here!" They were about five yards behind her. To see that rising sun badge on a beret again! It did us more good than anything we have experienced so far.

One fellow said he was "Bates, from Thornbury" and the other said he was "Gillam, from Perth", and the first thing we noticed, after their youth, was their very white teeth. We made these boys sit on our bali bali and then we fired our hundreds of questions.

We told them we had heard that "the King of America" was dead—this from a Chinese when we were out water-carrying one day. Did it mean Mr Roosevelt had died? Who won the war? Who won the football final in Melbourne? Will we be home for the Melbourne Cup? Is the Royal

Family O.K.? Is the *Queen Mary* still afloat? We were interested in this because most of us had sailed to Singapore in her in 1941. The answer came pat, "Yes, they both are." How and where are the 8th Division prisoners? Who is Prime Minister of Australia? Is Mr Churchill still Prime Minister of England? What are the latest songs? Australia could not have sent two men better equipped with all the answers. They told us of "swoon" men, and that Bing Crosby was the number one film star in Hollywood. Our remarks here were choice; we thought Bing was on the way out before we were ever taken prisoner. They told us of cold permanent waves, and we all thought we had better have one of those as soon as we could. They spoke of huge aeroplanes, "Liberators", "Boomerangs", "Mosquitoes", "B24's". We are hopelessly out of date and we can't think when we shall catch up with all the news of the last four years.

These two boys also told us of a bomb dropped on a Japanese city which killed thousands of people and reduced the place to a shambles. We were horrified to think one bomb could do that. They then said another similar bomb had been dropped on another Japanese city that did the same thing. What amazing progress has been made while we have been Rip Van Winkles!

13th September 1945. Two huge four-engined planes, the largest and most powerful we have ever seen, flew at tree-top height over us for nearly two hours this morning. We could see a man dressed in white standing in a doorway. What glorious planes they were! They were dropping parcels into the men's camp, we are told. The plane markings are different, white and blue, no red at all. It is such a thrill not to see that horrible red blob under the wings. There is quite a strong rumour in camp that they dropped *bread*! Wonder what bread tastes like? How marvellous!

14th September 1945. It was bread, and made at Cocos Island that day. We had half a slice each with *butter* and *Vegemite*, and it was like sponge cake. With it we had a bowl of cocoa, thick with sugar, and we all sat on the step in front of the hut at 7 p.m. and felt completely satisfied with life.

Quite a large quantity of food was dropped—boiled sweets, powdered milk, cheese, powdered egg, Vegemite, etc. Sealed dixies containing twenty-four hours' ration for one person were dropped. Hundreds of South East Asia Command news-papers, telling us about the war in Burma, were also dropped.

We are bartering with the natives the pieces of thin coloured material the Japs gave us. They are too "Tamil pink" for us. We are all making quite pretty nighties from the mosquito-net material given us last week. It is thick cotton material and would have made hot, airless nets. We are also bartering the Jap shirts and shorts, since we can't get them clean, for fruit, vegetables, eggs, chickens, and ducks. Dutchy comes every day, bringing his friends, and they do some of the bartering. We buy three chickens, alive, at 11 a.m. and have fried chicken for lunch at 1 p.m.! Chris, Flo, and I are the executioners. We have at least four visitors for lunch every day now, and are leading quite a social life.

The natives are looking quite smart in their khaki shorts and shirts bartered from this camp. They are so smart, in fact, that they look like our own people until we see that their faces are not familiar. We are certainly all the same colour! These natives are getting harder to deal with each day and must be doing quite well for themselves.

15th September 1945. Wilma and I are the family cooks today, since Dutchy did not come. Some girl bartered her material for a huge pile of real French beans! Jess Doyle could not resist some duck-eggs a native was trying to sell her. Jess was dressed in her old "Black Bottom" shorts, one of the seven pairs Win made from a nun's gown and now worn solidly for three years, which the native definitely had his eye on. He told her she could have five eggs for the shorts, so Jess, in a desperate moment, told him to *nanti* while she dashed inside and removed the shorts. Then somebody took them outside to the native and collected the eggs. Really, these natives should pull themselves together!

193

Chapter 25

17th September 1945. We are out of it! ! !

What a time we have had! We were rescued from that
hell-hole by our own R.A.A.F. and an Australian War Cor-
respondent, Haydon Lennard, who, after searching for us for
nearly two weeks, finally got in touch with the two Dutch
paratroops at Loebok Linggau. Their story would fill a book.
The Japanese would not help them or tell them where we
were.

At about 9.30 p.m. two nights ago we were all in bed, but
not asleep, when we heard Mrs Hinch saying from the doorway, "May I see you for a moment, Miss James?" We all
waited, thinking perhaps one of our girls up on the hill might
be very ill. Val, who was nearest the door, said in a hushed
voice, "Girls, I think she said we are going home tomorrow."

Immediately eight heads popped out from under the nets,
and great chatter went on.

Sister James came inside after a few minutes and said we had to be ready to go at 4 a.m.; we were to be flown out of Sumatra to Singapore. We could take one change of clothing, a blanket and pillow each only. What blankets? She told us this quietly, as if that kind of thing were said to us every day of our lives, but after a while we couldn't help getting terribly excited, and everybody started rushing round the place.

Iole was quite sick; she had been in hospital for two days with an abscess on her hip, so I went over to tell her and bring her back to the hut. Helen, a Scottish sister on duty there for the night, would not let me in.

I said to her, "But, Helen, we are flying to Singapore to-night."

Helen took some convincing. "Don't you dare waken the other patients!"

That was all right, but I could not waken Iole. In desperation I pulled her feet, the only part of her I could reach without waking those on either side of her, but she slept on. I went outside and asked Helen to waken her, telling her that I would be back in ten minutes, but I could not get any co-operation, you can't budge Scotswomen! She simply did not believe me. I can see her point, it did sound fantastic. However, finally we both got Iole awake and she staggered back with me to the hut.

Half an hour later the hospital was lighted up and everybody was awake and excited about our departure; we were going to take some of the sickest British patients with us.

We all decided to have a supper party, so invited the Charitas nuns from next door to come in for some coffee. They had been in bed, on the floor, for hours, but they all came in at our very special request, and all in their nightgowns, bless them.

Val and Blanchie soon had a huge fire going in our kitchen. None of us had ever seen such a blaze in our tiny stove at the back of our hut. They made about a gallon of black coffee, which we swamped with sugar, and fried some rice crust, which we made to look like toast and ate with Jap tinned meat.

What a satisfactory feeling to be able to offer our boiled sweets, dropped from the air that day, to everybody until they were all gone, knowing there would be more where we were going!

The nuns sang a Dutch song to us, wishing us all the very best and "long may we live in glory", and we sang to them. Then they went home while we tidied up the hut, giving away everything we owned, all our food and dress materials. It cut me to the quick to leave behind a cotton frock I had been making with the help of Jean Ashton. It was almost finished and ready to wear. The hours I had spent with a rusty needle and drawn threads for cotton, trying to put it together!

At 10 p.m. somebody appeared on the doorstep saying Sister James was *wanted on the phone*! What phone? Where is the phone? It did sound ridiculous, away out there in the rubber. However, she went up to the guard-house and there spoke to Flying Officer Brown, R.A.A.F., and he told her of the arrangements he and Mr Lennard had made to get us to the aerodrome at Lahat, about one hundred miles away.

This was the latest night we had had for years. There seemed to be plenty of things to do, and many farewells to make. Quite late that night our Australian friends, Mr Wooten and Mr McCann, arrived. They heard in their camp that we were going, so they came over at once to see us off. We gave them the remainder of our Jap shirts, shorts, and a pair of boots each. They could use these for bartering purposes until they themselves could get out.

At 1 a.m. we had breakfast and more coffee, then the rain came down with a vengeance. Visibility nil.

At 4.30 a.m. we set out in pitch darkness and pouring rain through mud, pools, in and out of drains, and so up to the guard-house on top of the hill.

We were taken into Loebok Linggau station in Japanese open trucks, driven by Tanaka and Amana. Sixty of us finally got away, we twenty-four sisters, and thirty-six other British, mainly nurses, including Scottish Helen, believing her ears at last. She was talking so fast and so excitedly with her Glasgow accent that nobody could understand her. Helen is a very amusing girl.

It took nearly three hours to travel the twelve miles to the railway station, since Amana saw to it that his truck broke down every half mile. He kept getting out and removing a piece of engine and throwing it into undergrowth on the side of the road. The two Dutch paratroops escorting us kept picking them up and handing them back to Amana, saying, "You may need this, George."

When daylight came and the rain stopped we were rescued by another truck, which had two couches in the back for us to sit on. Not a Nipponese idea, I'll bet! This truck soon landed us at the station, where we met many British and Dutch men who had managed to get into the town from their camp somehow, just to see there was not any funny business and that we got away safely.

At the station we were met by Haydon Lennard and Flying Officer Brown, one of our pilots, who had risked everything to get his plane down on the tiny Lahat aerodrome. He was not to know if the place was mined or not, or what kind of reception he would get from the Japanese. He landed so he could find out where the Australian sisters were. He had been advised not to land there, apparently, but thank goodness he did. The plane was taken back to Singapore after dropping him and Haydon Lennard, to return when the two men signalled for it.

The Indonesian train-driver would not start the train. More and more Japanese were arriving, and it was beginning to look a bit nasty. In desperation the men called to the train-driver to "take it away" and, when he did not understand, they said, "Sh-sh-sh-shshshsh", but that driver woulu not move an inch. It appears he had been driving the train to Lahat for years and had never started before 8 a.m., and, in spite of this being a special, he refused to start before 8 a.m.

this day! At last we started off, amid cheers and cheerios from the men and the most horrible expressions of hatred on the faces of the Japs gathered there. The contrast in expressions between the two groups of very different men was worth photographing.

We arrived at Lahat at midday, to be greeted with the news that only one plane taking thirty people could get across from Singapore, and that plane had not been sighted! So we sat in that hot train for about an hour, while Japanese officers, who spoke English, bowed and scraped and apologized, offering us rice and bully-beef, very sweet coffee, and tins of milk, which we ate and drank very quickly. It was a long time since our 1 a.m. breakfast.

In the meantime the most odd collection of natives appeared just outside the station and their expressions were anything but friendly. Haydon Lennard and Flying Officer Brown donned dark glasses and grim expressions and walked up and down that platform with their hands nonchalantly resting on their revolvers, and kept those Japanese officers running. Haydon Lennard even arranged for the Japs to get out of one of their large houses so we sixty could go there for the night, if necessary.

However, all was well. Thirty people were taken to a Dutch hospital, while we twenty-four and six others were taken to the aerodrome, once more sitting on couches in trucks. When we sighted the tiny aerodrome we thought we had better discard our old camp hats; such headgear never was seen in a civilized country, so we threw them into some bushes on our way.

At the aerodrome we were given chairs by the Japs there, and we sat in the shade under an attap roof, a small shelter shed really, and waited. Some of the girls spread their belongings on the grass and slept. At about three o'clock we heard the hum of an engine, all jumped up to find an old Jap truck reversing in the distance! Back to our chairs once more, then at about four o'clock we heard the plane, and then saw her come in over the hills and make a perfect landing. Oh, what joy!

A door opened, and out stepped two women dressed in grey who walked towards us. What a marvellous sight to see our good old army grey, but *slacks* in place of skirts! We realized once more how out of date we were, standing there in our forlorn uniforms patched with bits and pieces. As they came nearer we recognized Colonel Sage, our Matron-in-Chief, and Sister Floyd, one of the 2/10th A.G.H. girls who was with the party that managed to get away from Singapore just before us in February 1942.

Major Windsor, a doctor, also came towards us. We were thrilled to see them and tried to hurry towards them, but our legs would not carry us, so we stayed standing where we were.

How absolutely wonderful for our Matron-in-Chief to come all the way from Australia to Sumatra to get us! She, too, did not know how the Japanese would behave when their plane landed. They were all so brave. The last person to leave the plane was a R.A.A.F. nursing sister, a Queenslander, Sister Chandler, who knew many of our girls.

Major Windsor said an Australian hospital was ready in Singapore, a ward waiting for us. That was grand news; we were so tired and dirty and very anxious to get to bed. Just before we entered the plane we met the pilot, who grinned and said, "Call me Fred", and he had a chat with us.

Colonel Sage and Sister Floyd went into Lahat and stayed at the hospital for the night to look after the thirty people we left behind that day. They were all to be flown to Singapore next morning.

Our flight out of Sumatra was a joy, though we were terribly tired. To leave that country behind us was all we asked.

We arrived at Singapore at dusk. Cameras, reporters, Red Cross helpers from England and Australia, biscuits, soap, tea, cigarettes, all were there. We even had our tea in a cup with a saucer! How filthy and untidy and shabby we looked amongst all these beautifully uniformed people, but why worry? We were out at last.

The Red Cross people were wonderful to us. They helped us to walk over to a building and carried our few miserable belongings, which up to that moment we had thought fairly respectable.

We were then driven in ambulances out to St Patrick's College, where the new Australian hospital was. This same place was the 13th A.G.H. in 1941 and early 1942. So the 13th A.G.H. members of our group had retraced their steps right back to the place they were forced to leave in February 1942!

Our welcome at this hospital was wonderful. We were very soon surrounded by the familiar faces of nurses we knew so well, but not one of us could remember their names! They were friends we had known for years, but for the life of us we could not think what to call them.

Somebody told the 13th A.G.H. girls that their orderlies had buried their cabin trunks full of clothes and personal belongings before they were sent away by the Japs in 1942, but the Japs had built a two-storey wing over the very spot, and we were to be nursed on the top floor of that very wing!

I was too tired to remember much, but I do remember being helped upstairs and taken to a brightly lighted ward, spotlessly clean—no mud floors here—and huge white beds with white sheets and two large pillows; a bed each. It took all I knew to stop myself from bursting into tears.

We then proceeded to the bathroom, where we had the good old Singapore "stand-up" bath, plenty of water now, and pretty silk or cotton pyjamas to put on. These were given to us by the sisters of this hospital, also talc powder, a tooth-brush and paste. After our bath we had our first meal in civilization, a lonely-looking poached egg and a cup of tea. It was not enough; we were very hungry, but extremely happy.

Then we met our friends on the hospital staff, for a social chat this time. They were girls with whom we had trained, some girls from whom we were separated in Singapore in 1942 and who got home after that—what a wonderful welcome!

At last we went to bed, but hardly anyone slept; we were far too comfortable! A soft bed after three and a half years of tiled floors and uneven bali balis was too much.

25th September 1945. This is the life. We are staying here for a few weeks before we leave for Australia, either by plane or hospital ship. It is a good idea. None of us wanted to arrive home looking as we did. Already there is a great improvement, many of the girls looking quite pretty.

The sisters on the staff are being simply wonderful. As well as nursing us they have given us more pyjamas, slippers, house-coats, pretty skirts, pretty blouses, clothes of all descriptions, powders and creams, etc. Actually our skins do not look so bad now the first few layers of camp are off. These things were given to us as soon as they sighted the rubbish we brought from Sumatra.

The day after we arrived reporters and photographers were given their heads for an hour. What an hour! We were very pleased to be able to broadcast a message home, and as we were still very excited we all seemed to say such silly things, nevertheless it was fun.

We are all gaining pounds in weight daily. My five stone has gone to six and a half in a week. We weigh three times each day and it is never the same. We hope this weight stops going on when it should!

The hospital is full of A.I.F. prisoners and those who can come and visit us. Most of them are from Changi. We all seem to have plenty to say and, on comparing notes, we find the Japs must have treated all prisoners alike. These men send us dozens of eggs, cooked chicken, bananas, and even raisins. We keep telling them not to worry, there is plenty to eat here.

Cables and letters from home have arrived and are still arriving. This time they are only a few weeks old, such a change from Japanese mail. We have all caught up on our home news now.

Miss Sage came in to see us, and a day or so ago had a long talk with us about the activities of the A.A.N.S. while we were in Sumatra. What an interesting war we have missed! It was rather fun to be called "girls" again, when most of us felt like old hags.

Yesterday we tasted beer for the first time for years. A padre gave it to us, and it was iced. It was nectar of the gods.

Our friends and the Red Cross girls here are still bringing us pretty things we have not seen for years. The Red Cross has provided us with things we have done without for so long—towels, face washers, dressing-gowns, pyjamas, brushes, combs, mirrors, etc. The first thing I saw when I opened my Red Cross box was a nail file, which was the first thing I missed as I swam through those mangrave swamps in 1942 when I realized that I had lost everything I owned.

1st October 1945. We were taken out to the new P.O.W. Reception Centre at Changi today and saw and met Gracie Fields. She was giving the men a concert. She was wonderful and had us all in fits of laughter. We loved listening to her pianist, too; we haven't heard a piano played like that for years.

3rd October 1945. We gave a sherry party to the sisters and officers of 14th A.G.H. here last night. We also invited a few Australian paratroops we had met, and our pilots, Squadron Leader Madsen and Flying Officer Brown, also Haydon Lennard. We all wore borrowed frocks and really looked anything but internees. Unfortunately, just as the party seemed to start, we were all sent back to bed. Fine hostesses we made! We need not have worried; sounds coming over from the direction of the mess indicated that the party went on for ages.

4th October 1945. We sail for Australia tomorrow in the Hospital Ship *Manunda*. At the moment we are flat out trying on borrowed grey safari jackets and slacks, army shoes and hats. We feel as if we have an awful lot of clothes on after wearing shorts and sun-tops for so long.

10th October 1945. At sea, and well on our way home at last. We sat on board for three days before we left Singapore.

All the things we have been wanting for so long we had in the first two days on board—lamb's fry, steak, Irish stew, oxtail, fresh apples. We are right now, none of us will ever be food-conscious or hungry again.

23rd October 1945. Still at sea. We have been on Australia and left it again. We saw our first little piece of it at about 3 p.m. last Thursday, when the deck rails were lined with hundreds of soldiers and us twenty-four nurses. We were terribly excited at first, but as it got nearer silence reigned. For an hour we watched Fremantle getting closer and still there was silence everywhere. Iole and Mickey Syer were to leave us here, the port of Perth. Extraordinarily enough, Iole and I had nothing to say to each other except, "You will be home tonight, how does it feel?" and her reply, "I wonder if my family will be on the wharf."

When the ship was only a few yards off the wharf the dinner gong sounded, but nobody was interested in anything else but those hundreds of Perth people standing and cheering on the wharf and that wonderful Matron-in-Chief of ours, Colonel Sage, standing down there waiting to welcome us home to Australia. How thrilled we all were to see her waving to us!

When the *Manunda* eventually tied up people came on board laden with the most glorious flowers and fruit—arms full of them. First on deck, I think, was Iole's mother, but Iole could not be found. After she saw her family on the wharf she went to her cabin and started to pack again. I might add she had been packing all day!

We were taken out to the Military Hospital at Hollywood and our reception there was unforgettable. Flowers were everywhere, even on the ceilings; such arrangement of flowers we have never seen before, mostly red, white, and blue. Apparently they had broadcast for flowers and they came from every garden in Perth and kept on coming.

Once more we met many more people we knew. For some time I was talking with a friend of mine who had come to meet me there. After a while Pat Gunther and Pat Blake joined in with, "We are so sorry to interrupt, we have been waiting here for ages for Jeff to introduce us, but we do want to say now we love your pretty blue hat!"

I went home with Iole and her family that night, and we each had our first hot bath for nearly four years. The baths on the ship were cold salt-water ones, so this was the real thing at last.

We left Perth for Melbourne next day, having been given skirts and stockings to wear in place of slacks. That feels better.

We arrive in Melbourne tomorrow, and my four catty Sydney friends have bet me that it will be raining.

24th October 1945, 5 p.m. It *is* raining! We are due in Melbourne in one hour; it is wet and cold, visibility nil; my Sydney friends are grinning all over their faces. They expected it. . . . Well, here it is, and I'm proud of it.

BANGKOK

THAILAND

SAIGON

"VYNER BROC

SOUTH CHINA
SEA

MALAYA
MALACCA

SINGAPORE

SUMATRA

SARAWAK

BORNEO

BANKA
IS.

MUNTOK

PALEMBANG

LAHAT

LOEBOK LINGGAU

JAVA SEA

JAVA

C

INDIAN OCEAN

0   200   400   600 MILES

DEL R D 1947